BL: 4.6 —
AR Pts: 4.0
Quiz No. 172477

MVFOL

THE GRIFFIN'S RIDDLE

THE IMAGINARY VETERINARY: BOOK 5

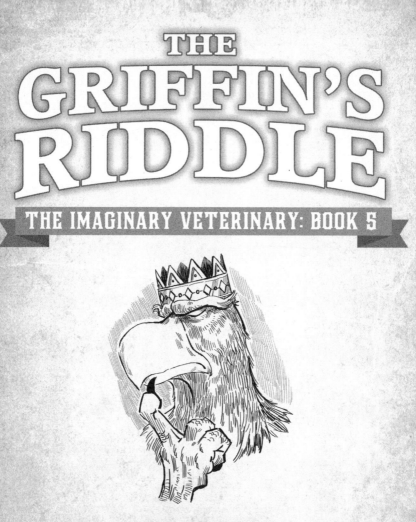

BY SUZANNE SELFORS
ILLUSTRATIONS BY DAN SANTAT

Little, Brown and Company
New York Boston

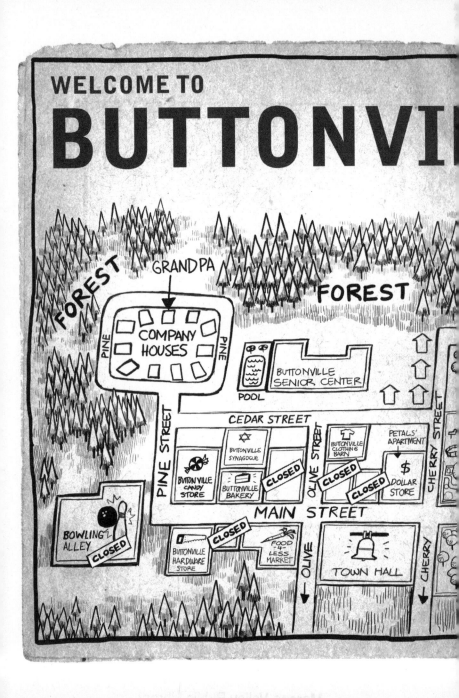

Little, Brown and Company

Hachette Book Group
1290 Avenue of the Americas, New York, NY 10104
Visit us at lb-kids.com

Little, Brown and Company is a division of Hachette Book Group, Inc.
The Little, Brown name and logo are trademarks of Hachette Book Group, Inc.

The publisher is not responsible for websites (or their content) that are not owned by the publisher.

First Edition: February 2015

Library of Congress Cataloging-in-Publication Data

Selfors, Suzanne.
  The griffin's riddle / by Suzanne Selfors ; illustrations by Dan Santat.
    pages cm.—(The imaginary veterinary ; book 5)
  Summary: "Ten-year-olds Pearl and Ben, continuing their apprenticeships at Dr. Woo's Worm Hospital, discover that Dr. Woo and the sasquatch are both sick with Troll Tonsillitis, and they must travel to the Imaginary World to find the only cure: a griffin's feather"—Provided by publisher.
  ISBN 978-0-316-28690-9 (hardback)—ISBN 978-0-316-28688-6 (ebook)—
ISBN 978-0-316-28689-3 (library edition ebook) [1. Griffins—Fiction. 2. Imaginary creatures—Fiction. 3. Veterinarians—Fiction. 4. Apprentices—Fiction.] I. Title.
  PZ7.S456922Gr 2015
  [Fic]—dc23

                                  2014029157

                        10 9 8 7 6 5 4 3 2 1

                                  RRD-C

                  Printed in the United States of America

ALSO BY SUZANNE SELFORS:

The Imaginary Veterinary Series

The Sasquatch Escape

The Lonely Lake Monster

The Rain Dragon Rescue

The Order of the Unicorn

Ever After High

Next Top Villain

General Villainy: A Destiny Do-Over Diary

The Smells Like Dog Series

Smells Like Dog

Smells Like Treasure

Smells Like Pirates

To Catch a Mermaid

Fortune's Magic Farm

For griffins everywhere

CONTENTS

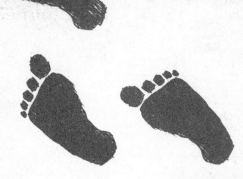

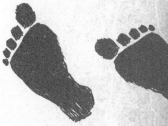

1

BOARD GAME DAY

Ben Silverstein's bottom had gone numb.

He'd been sitting in a cold metal chair for two hours, playing checkers. In Ben's opinion, checkers was one of the most boring games ever invented, right up there with Go Fish and dominos. No laser cannons, no high-speed chases, no flashing lights or sirens. Just a wooden board, a pile of red buttons, and a pile of black buttons. It was like playing a game from the caveman days.

And to make matters worse, Ben's opponent was Mrs. Froot, the oldest person in Buttonville. Her hair was so white it looked as if snow had fallen on her head. Her hearing aids were so squeaky it sounded as if two mice were living in her ears. And her eyeglass lenses were so thick that if a sunbeam shot through them, the whole senior center would catch fire. Ben secretly wished that would happen because it would give him an excuse to stop playing.

It was Tuesday, which was board game day at the Buttonville Senior Center. Ben didn't have anything else to do, so he'd agreed to spend the morning with his grandfather and the rest of the seniors. The air was stuffy with perfumes and medicated ointments.

"You're a good boy," his grandfather Abe Silverstein said from the next table, where he was playing Battleship with Mr. Filbert. "Isn't my grandson a good boy to play eleven games of checkers with Mrs. Froot?"

"King me!" Mrs. Froot commanded, strands of hair slipping from her bun.

"Yeah, okay," Ben grumbled, placing a red button on top of another red button. As it turned out, Mrs.

Froot was a bit of a ninja when it came to checkers. She had three kings on the board while Ben had zero.

Grandpa Abe leaned sideways and nudged Ben with his elbow. "How come you look so sad?"

"He's a sore loser," Mr. Filbert said. A military veteran, he'd come prepared for Battleship, dressed in his army jacket and medals. "No one likes to lose. If I don't take my pills, I lose my memory."

"I'm not sad about *losing*," Ben said, which was the truth. In the grand scheme of things, losing eleven games of checkers wasn't important. But some of the other things that had happened that summer were *definitely* important.

Like becoming an apprentice at Dr. Woo's Worm Hospital.

Thankfully, Dr. Woo didn't really take care of worms. Behind the walls of the old Buttonville Button Factory, Dr. Woo took care of Imaginary creatures. Only one week into his apprenticeship, Ben had already met a wyvern hatchling, a black dragon, a rain dragon, a leprechaun, a lake monster, a kelpie, two unicorns, and a sasquatch. And even though yesterday's apprenticeship hadn't introduced any new creatures, just an entire day spent plucking slugs from the sasquatch's fur, it had still been way

better than sitting around playing old-fashioned board games.

But despite the great adventures in the Imaginary World, Ben couldn't forget the reason why his parents had sent him to stay with his grandfather in Buttonville. They needed time alone to discuss some "troubles." And that very morning, before heading to the senior center, Ben had received some bad news.

When Ben returned to Los Angeles at the end of the summer, his dad would be living in a different house. And that was the real reason why Ben felt sad.

"*Oy vey!*" Grandpa Abe exclaimed. "You sank my battleship!"

Four games later, Mrs. Froot dozed off in her chair. The checkers marathon was finally over.

"I'm pooped," Grandpa Abe said. "I need a nap, too." He put on his canvas hat and grabbed his cane. Then he waved good-bye to his friends. Once he and Ben were outside, he wrapped an arm around Ben's shoulder. "Listen to me, boychik. You have some big changes coming your way. What's important to

remember is that your mother and your father will love you just as much in two houses as in one house. Sometimes things stay the same, sometimes they change. This is life!"

Ben knew his parents would still love him. But he didn't know how he'd feel having two bedrooms and two bus stops. It sounded very confusing.

Grandpa Abe's cane tapped as they walked down the front steps. "I know what you need to make you feel better. You need a big bowl of my matzo ball soup. It cures everything—common cold, influenza, even sadness. What's better than a fat matzo ball?"

"Okay," Ben said. He'd always liked matzo ball soup, but he didn't believe for a moment that it could cure his sad feelings.

"Ben!" a voice called.

"Hi, Pearl!" he called back.

A girl ran up the walkway, toward the senior center, her blond ponytail bouncing against her neck. "I ran all the way here," she explained, her cheeks bright red. "We've got a huge problem!"

2

WORM TROUBLE

Pearl Petal tended to get excited about things. Ben had only known her for a short time, but he'd already figured out that she wasn't the kind of girl who liked to sit quietly and watch life pass by. Her curiosity got her into trouble now and then, but that didn't stop her. She asked questions. She stepped boldly into the unknown. She was the most adventurous kid Ben had ever met.

Because Pearl also worked as an apprentice to

Dr. Woo, she and Ben shared a big batch of secrets. So when she hollered, "We've got a huge problem," his heart missed a beat.

"What's the matter?" Ben asked as Pearl skidded to a stop right in front of him. She stood so close that the toes of her sneakers touched his.

"You look like you've seen a ghost," Grandpa Abe said.

Ben wasn't worried about ghosts. Ghosts weren't real. But it was entirely possible that Pearl had seen something else, like a three-headed dog, a yeti, or a cyclops. Those things *were* real. Had something dangerous escaped the hospital, like the nasty child-eating kelpie they'd met in the basement pool?

"It...it...it wasn't a ghost." A big wad of gum appeared between Pearl's teeth as she chewed as fast as a squirrel. She glanced worriedly at Ben's grandfather. He didn't know any of their secrets. In fact, they'd been careful not to reveal their secrets to *anyone*. "Mrs. Mulberry was just at the store," Pearl explained. Pearl's family owned the Buttonville

Dollar Store. "She bought a little box so she could carry her worm."

"Martha Mulberry has a worm?" Grandpa Abe asked with surprise.

"She has a whole bunch of them," Pearl said, fidgeting as if there were ants in her shoes. "But one of them is sick."

Ben furrowed his brow. This was very worrisome news. Mrs. Mulberry, president of the Buttonville Welcome Wagon Committee, was the snoopiest person in town. She'd ordered red compost worms from a fancy gardening catalog, not because she owned a compost bin, but because she wanted an excuse to meet Dr. Woo. The only way to get inside Dr. Woo's hospital was to become an apprentice or to possess a sick worm that needed care.

"She's going to Dr. Woo's right now!" Pearl cried, squeezing Ben's arm so hard he thought it might snap in two.

"Ow," Ben said.

"Sorry." Pearl released her grip. "I'm just so worried. We have to stop her."

"Why would you keep Mrs. Mulberry from seeing Dr. Woo?" Grandpa Abe asked with a wag of his
finger. "A sick worm should go to a worm doctor."

Ben's grandfather didn't understand what was
at stake. If Martha Mulberry got inside the hospital, she'd ruin everything. She'd tell the whole
world that Dr. Woo had a Portal into the Imaginary
World. Dr. Woo would have to move to another town
and leave Ben and Pearl behind!

Pearl stared at Ben, her green eyes super wide. He knew that look. She wanted him to make up a story. Ben wasn't a soccer star or a computer genius, but he did excel at one thing—creative storytelling. Some might call it *lying*.

Ben gathered his thoughts. He imagined Mrs. Mulberry storming the hospital, the way an invader might storm a castle. She'd pillage the whole place, looking in every corner, not for gold or jewels, but for information. Gossip was her career. He looked up at his grandfather and delivered an explanation. "We want to stop Mrs. Mulberry because we...we don't want to miss the worm examination. We're Dr. Woo's apprentices, so we need to learn as much as possible. That's our job."

"Yep," Pearl said with an eager nod. "It's our job."

Grandpa Abe shrugged. "My grandson, the future worm doctor. This I never expected." He pointed his cane down the sidewalk. "Well, what are you waiting for? Hurry!"

Like horses released from the starting gate, Ben

and Pearl raced away. Pearl took the lead, as usual, her shiny basketball shorts flapping against her knees.

"I'll keep the soup warm for you," Grandpa Abe called.

"Thanks!" Ben called back.

Ben followed Pearl down Cedar Street and onto Cherry. They ran along the park, then took a right onto Maple, passing the duck pond and the closed gas station. Tall trees lined the road as it cut through the forest. Ben's side started to ache, but he wasn't about to complain. This was a million times better than playing checkers. He and Pearl were on a mission to protect Dr. Woo's secrets! One more bend in the road and they'd be able to see the hospital.

"Whoa!" Pearl cried as a yellow tennis ball rolled across her path, nearly tripping her.

If Ben had been back home in Los Angeles, he would have assumed that the ball had escaped from a tennis court or a golden retriever's mouth. But this

was Buttonville, which was *nothing* like home. Ben stumbled, then grabbed the ball. It was drenched in something slimy.

"Slobber," he realized. Then he looked around and gasped. A huge head stuck out of the forest.

And it belonged to a dragon.

3

A little over a week ago, Ben might have fainted at the sight of a dragon squatting at the edge of a forest. But at the time, Ben had believed that dragons existed only in storybooks. Now he knew the truth.

This particular dragon was as wide as a Cadillac and covered in black scales. He had four legs, a pair of wings, and a mouth filled with sharp, serrated teeth. Although the dragon was capable of spouting fire and melting metal, Ben wasn't one bit afraid. "Hi, Metalmouth," Ben said as he and Pearl ran up to the friendly beast.

"Hiya, Ben. Hiya, Pearl." Branches swayed as the dragon thumped his long tail. A gray feather was stuck between two of his sharp teeth. Metalmouth liked eating pigeons. His eyes widened as he spied the tennis ball in Ben's hand. "You wanna play fetch? Huh? Wanna?" His tongue popped out and he started panting.

"We shouldn't," Pearl told him. "Someone might see you."

"Aw, please," Metalmouth begged, his tail thumping again.

Ben couldn't resist. The dragon was the closest he'd come to having a dog. "Just one toss," Ben said as he threw the ball back into the forest. Metalmouth bounded after it, shaking the ground like an earthquake and breaking only a few trees in the process. Ben and Pearl followed him deeper into the forest, away from the road in case any cars drove past. During the day, Metalmouth was usually asleep in his nest on the hospital roof. If Mrs. Mulberry saw him, she'd call the zoo!

The dragon dropped the ball at Ben's feet. "You wanna play again? Huh?"

"Metalmouth, what are you doing out here?" Pearl asked.

"I came to tell you something." He tucked the tennis ball behind one of his scales. A loud crunch sounded as he sat on a huckleberry bush. "Mr. Tabby's canceling your apprenticeship." Mr. Tabby was Dr. Woo's assistant.

"Canceling?" Ben gulped. "Forever?"

"Not forever. Just for tomorrow."

"Did I do something wrong?" Pearl asked. "I don't think I broke any more rules. But I might have. I'm not sure."

"Mr. Tabby doesn't want you at the hospital tomorrow, because..." The dragon took a deep, wheezy breath. "Because..." He opened his mouth so wide the kids could see his uvula. Then he sneezed. A gale-force wind roared over Ben and Pearl, coating them with dragon germs and nearly knocking them off their feet. The pigeon feather came loose, too.

"Eeew," Pearl said, scrunching her nose. Metalmouth's breath wasn't worse than a dog's— there was just a lot more of it.

Ben wiped his face with his sleeve. "Are you sick?"

"No," the dragon said with a frown. "Dr. Woo is sick, but not me. I'm not..." He took another deep breath. This time, both Ben and Pearl covered their faces as the sneeze blew over their heads. "Uh-oh," Metalmouth said, his shoulders sagging. "I don't wanna be sick. I don't wanna take medicine." He might have descended from a long line of ferocious, village-burning beasts, but Metalmouth was a big baby at heart.

"What kind of sick?" Ben asked uneasily. "A cold? Or the flu?"

"I had the flu once," Pearl said. "It felt like a Martian was living in my stomach."

"Is it contagious?" Ben asked worriedly. "Will I need to get a shot?" While Ben didn't mind taking medicine, he really hated getting injections. He'd had a whole series of them on account of his allergies.

"A shot?" Metalmouth said, his ears flattening.

Pearl patted his paw. "Maybe you won't need medicine or a shot. How long does this thing last?"

"I don't know." Metalmouth shrugged. "Mr. Tabby said the sickness came from the Imaginary World. And we have to be careful we don't give it to any of the humans in Buttonville. That's why Mr. Tabby canceled for tomorrow. He wanted me to warn you not to come to the hospital." Then he coughed.

It was a full-frontal germ bath!

"Uh, thanks for the warning," Ben said. He didn't want to hurt the dragon's feelings by pointing out that he and Pearl would probably be stricken with the mysterious illness, thanks to that dose of dragon mucus. Ben could practically feel the germs squirming their way up his nose and down into his lungs.

"I'm not afraid of getting sick," Pearl said, jutting out her chin. "Besides, we have to go to the hospital because we're on an important mission. Mrs. Mulberry has a sick worm. We've got to keep her from getting inside so she doesn't see anything she's not supposed to see."

"You mean the loud lady who's standing at the front gate?" Metalmouth asked, steam wafting from his nostrils. "She's *scary*."

It was sort of funny to think that a huge dragon could be frightened of a small woman like Mrs. Mulberry, but Ben didn't laugh. Metalmouth was only ten years old in human years—the same age as Ben and Pearl. Even Ben felt a bit frightened of Mrs. Mulberry. "She won't hurt you," Ben assured

Metalmouth as he patted the dragon's other front paw. "But it's super important you don't let her see you because she'll tell everyone."

"Yeah," Pearl said. *"Everyone."*

Metalmouth frowned. "That would be bad. Whenever people find out about me and Dr. Woo, we have to move. I don't want to move again."

"I wouldn't want to move, either," Pearl said. "I've lived above the Dollar Store all my life. No other place would feel like home."

Ben cringed at the word *home*, remembering the morning's phone call.

"Whenever I get sad about moving, Dr. Woo tells me that home isn't a place. It's a state of mind." Metalmouth scratched behind his ear. "I don't really know what that means."

What does that mean? Ben wondered. For him, home was definitely a place. It was located in Los Angeles, and it had five bedrooms, an outdoor pizza oven, and a swimming pool.

"You won't have to move," Ben assured him.

"You can count on us," Pearl said. "We'll get rid of Mrs. Mulberry."

"I sure hope so." Metalmouth tossed back his head and coughed again. The shock wave knocked pinecones off nearby trees.

"You should go to bed and rest," Pearl told him. "I mean, go to your *nest* and rest."

"Okay. But I still don't want to take any medicine." Metalmouth unfurled his wings, and after much flapping and the breaking of more branches, he rose toward the sky.

Ben and Pearl ran back to the road. Now they had two worries. They needed to stop Mrs. Mulberry, *and* they needed to stay healthy. Was that a tickle at the back of Ben's throat? Did his forehead feel hot already? "If I get some kind of weird disease, my parents are going to freak out," he said, trying his best to keep up with Pearl. He didn't want to think about the possibility that he'd be sent back home to Los Angeles to see Dr. Rosenbaum, his pediatrician. Dr. Rosenbaum always pounded Ben's knees

with a rubber hammer and stared into Ben's eye-balls with a small flashlight.

And gave shots!

Ben and Pearl raced the rest of the way down Maple Street, until they reached the dead end at the old button factory gate.

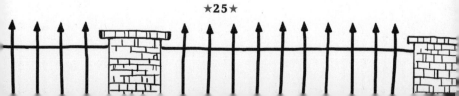

4

The Buttonville Button Factory had closed many years ago, leaving most of the townspeople without jobs. After the closure, the ten-story building had stood unused and abandoned. But now it was home to Dr. Woo's Worm Hospital. The doctor had made no exterior changes—windows were still broken, paint was still peeling, and the lawn was still choked with weeds. One patch had recently grown two stories high, having been fertilized by a pile of dragon dung Pearl had thrown off the roof. It wasn't a pretty setting—no one stopped to take photos and say, "Oh, how lovely. This should be on the cover of a magazine." But it had turned out to be a great place to hide a dragon, a sasquatch, and lots of other creatures, thanks to the tall wrought-iron fence that surrounded the property, and the locked gate that kept out anyone with a snoopy disposition.

"We're not too late," Ben said as he and Pearl stopped running.

Although her back was turned, it was easy to identify Mrs. Mulberry because she always wore her Welcome Wagon uniform—a pair of red overalls and a red baseball cap. With her was her daughter, Victoria Mulberry. Victoria was ten years old and also dressed in red overalls and a red baseball cap. Both mother and daughter possessed the reddest, frizziest hair Ben had ever seen.

"Yoo-hoo!" Mrs. Mulberry hollered, her face pressed against the padlocked gate. "I have a sick worm! I demand to see Dr. Woo!"

"Mom, just climb over the fence," Victoria said. She was sitting in a red wagon, a book in her hands.

"Climb over?" Mrs. Mulberry snorted. "How am I supposed to do that, *Victoria*? The tips are pointy. Do you want your mother to get impaled?" She was right. The tops of the fence were as sharp as spears. Ben and Pearl knew a secret spot where it was safe to climb, but they weren't about to share that information.

Mrs. Mulberry set her little worm box on the ground. Then, with each hand gripping a metal bar, she shook the gate. "Yoo-hoo!" She shook it again. The gate shuddered from the brute force. Good thing she didn't have a battering ram or she'd bust right through!

Ben and Pearl eyed the little box. "Maybe we should grab it and go," Pearl whispered. Ben wasn't sure if that was a good idea. Two weeks ago, they'd trapped Mrs. Mulberry in a sasquatch-catching net, but they'd never tried to outrun her. He wiped a drop of sweat off his nose. Was he perspiring from the sunshine, or could this be the first sign that he was getting sick?

Victoria was busy reading, so she hadn't noticed Ben and Pearl standing at the sidewalk's edge. Cautiously, they took a step, then another, reaching out their hands. If they could get the worm box, then they could put a stop to this whole predicament.

Mrs. Mulberry whipped around and sneered at them. "What are *you two* doing here?"

It was a good thing Mrs. Mulberry had turned around, because at that moment, a dark shape flew across the sky and landed on the hospital's roof. Then the shape disappeared behind a cluster of tall chimneys. Ben exhaled with relief. Metalmouth was safe in his nest, and Mrs. Mulberry was none the wiser.

"I asked you a question," Mrs. Mulberry said huffily. "What are you doing here?"

"Work," Pearl blurted.

"Yeah, work," Ben said, sticking his hands into his jean pockets.

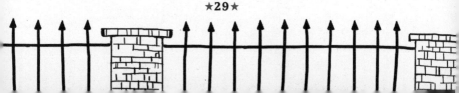

"They're fibbing." Victoria peered over the top of her book. "They work on Mondays, Wednesdays, and Fridays. Today is Tuesday." She wore a full set of blue braces and tended to spit when she spoke.

"We heard you have a sick worm, so we came to help," Ben said. "You don't have to bother Dr. Woo. Pearl and I know all about worms."

"Bother?" Mrs. Mulberry set her hands on her hips. "Why would I be *bothering* Dr. Woo? She's supposed to take care of worms. It says so right there." She pointed to the sign that hung on the front gate.

WELCOME TO DR. WOO'S WORM HOSPITAL.
DR. WOO DOES NOT TREAT CATS, DOGS, PIGS, RATS,
SNAKES, TURTLES, FISH, FROGS, OR ANY
OTHER CREATURE THAT IS NOT A WORM.
DR. WOO SEES WORMS BY APPOINTMENT ONLY.
IF YOU DON'T HAVE AN APPOINTMENT,
KEEP OUT!

"Yes that's true, but..." Ben couldn't tell them that Dr. Woo was sick with something that didn't even come from this world. He pointed down the long driveway, where a sign was taped to the hospital's front door. "Dr. Woo can't see you today, because the hospital is closed."

THE WORM HOSPITAL IS **CLOSED** UNTIL IT IS **OPEN**.

"That sign is always on the door," Mrs. Mulberry said. "What I'd like to know is, how can a hospital be closed every day of the week? That doesn't make sense." She folded her arms tightly and scowled at the apprentices. "Is there a reason you're trying to keep me from going inside?"

Pearl chewed her gum extra fast. Ben's toes

fidgeted. There were dozens of reasons. Like the switchboard operator named Violet, who was half person, half goat. And the magical Portal that traveled to the Imaginary World. And the yellow fairy dust that clung to Dr. Woo's hair.

"We're just trying to help," Ben said.

Pearl forced a big, fake smile, showing the gap between her front teeth. "If you give us the sick worm, Ben and I will take care of it for you."

Everyone looked down at the box. *How sick is the little creature?* Ben wondered. He and Pearl had actually never cared for a worm. They'd flea-bathed a sasquatch, they'd cured a lake monster's loneliness, and they'd mended a rain dragon's wound. Everyone thought Ben and Pearl were *worm* apprentices, but neither of them had encountered a worm inside Dr. Woo's hospital. They'd never done anything worm-oriented.

And yet, how difficult could it be? Worms were simple creatures, right?

Mrs. Mulberry grabbed the box. "It's my job as the president of the Welcome Wagon Committee to

interrogate, I mean, to *meet* everyone who moves to our town. That includes Dr. Woo." She whipped around and faced the gate again. "Yoo-hoo! Let me in!"

Pearl pulled Ben aside and whispered, "What do we do?" But before Ben could come up with a suggestion, Victoria scrambled out of the wagon, then elbowed her way between Ben and Pearl.

"I know there's a dragon living on that roof," Victoria said, keeping her voice low so her mom wouldn't hear. "I've seen it and I know it's real."

Ben and Pearl said nothing. They glanced at each other, eyes narrowed. Neither of them trusted Victoria.

"If you want to keep secrets from my mom, then you'll need my help," Victoria told them as she adjusted her glasses. "But my help will cost you." She leaned closer. "I want to meet the dragon."

Ben gulped. Unfortunately, exactly one week ago, Metalmouth had paid a daytime visit to the roof of Buttonville's Town Hall. Most of the residents had been inside the hall, attending a meeting, but Victoria had come out just in time to see Metalmouth fly away. Of course, both Ben and Pearl had denied the dragon's existence. But Victoria wasn't stupid. She knew a dragon when she saw one.

Pearl put her hands on her hips and glared at Victoria. "You can't blackmail me, Victoria Mulberry! I'm not scared of you."

Ben cleared his throat. "What Pearl meant to say is that dragons aren't real. You imagined the whole thing."

Victoria jutted out her chin. "Fine. Be that way. But you're going to regret this." She grabbed the gate and began shaking it. "Let us in! Let us in!" Mrs. Mulberry joined her.

Things were taking a turn for the worse. Ben wasn't sure how to get the Mulberrys away from the hospital. He needed a good story, and he needed it fast.

But then he froze. Pearl froze, too. Mrs. Mulberry and Victoria stopped shouting.

The front door to the hospital had opened!

5

VICTORIA THE SNEAK

Ben and Pearl held their breath, waiting to see who or *what* would emerge from the hospital's front door. Ben stood as stiff as a starched collar. An imaginary clock ticked in his head. Pearl wasn't moving, either, which, until that very moment, Ben had thought impossible. What would happen next?

A man stepped onto the front stoop.

"What's Mr. Tabby doing here?" Pearl whispered. "I thought Tuesday was his day off."

Mr. Tabby was dressed in his usual work attire—a crisp white shirt, perfectly pressed black trousers, and polished shoes. A green striped vest completed the outfit. He always reminded Ben of a butler. His long red hair was pulled back in a ponytail, like Pearl's, only tidier. As he strode down the gravel driveway, his gaze remained fixed upon the front gate.

"He looks angry," Pearl said from the corner of her mouth.

Mr. Tabby always looked grumpy, so his serious expression didn't worry Ben. However, the ring of keys that dangled from Mr. Tabby's left hand had caught Ben's attention. Was he going to unlock the padlock and let the Mulberrys inside?

Upon reaching the gate, Mr. Tabby turned his yellow-eyed gaze to Mrs. Mulberry. "You hollered?" he asked, his upper lip curling into a sneer.

"What does a person have to do to get some help around here?" Mrs. Mulberry complained. "I have a very sick worm."

"Is that so?" His red mustache, which was waxed into sections, twitched like a cat's whiskers. Mrs. Mulberry held the box up to the gate. Mr. Tabby sniffed the air. "I detect the odor of an ordinary red compost worm."

"That's right," Mrs. Mulberry said. "I got a whole shipment of them. But this one's not wiggling like the others." She clutched the box tightly, as if she'd never possessed anything more valuable in her entire life. She'd been trying to get inside that hospital all week, and this was her golden ticket.

Ben wanted to ask about Dr. Woo. How sick was she? Was it serious? But that couldn't be discussed in front of the Mulberrys. Mr. Tabby glanced at Pearl. "Do I also detect cinnamon gum?"

"Oops." Gum was not allowed inside the hospital. Pearl spat it into a clump of weeds.

"I want to see Dr. Woo," Mrs. Mulberry demanded.

Mr. Tabby carefully smoothed one of his mustache sections. Then, very slowly, he unlocked the padlock.

"Wait! Are you...?" Ben couldn't believe it. "Are you letting them in?"

"Yay!" Victoria cheered as the gate swung open. She grabbed her wagon and started to pull it through, but Mr. Tabby blocked her with an outstretched hand. "I must first verify that the patient is ill."

Mrs. Mulberry's cheeks turned as red as her overalls. "You don't believe me?"

"It is not a matter of belief, my dear woman. It is a matter of proof. Dr. Woo's days are quite busy, and it is my duty to make certain that she does not waste her time tending to a *healthy* worm." He tapped a long fingernail on the box. "If you'd be so kind."

Mrs. Mulberry opened the box. Mr. Tabby reached into his vest pocket and removed a monocle, which he placed over his left eye. The thick lens magnified his strange moon-shaped iris. Ben and Pearl stepped closer to get a better look. The little worm lay on the bottom of the box.

"Is it dead?" Pearl asked.

"On the contrary," Mr. Tabby said. He plucked an ivy leaf from one of the vines that grew up the fence, then shook it gently into the box. Drops of dew fell from the leaf and landed on the worm. The little critter began to wiggle.

"Was it thirsty?" Ben asked.

"Worms require moisture. They absorb it through their skin. If no moisture is provided, they dry up and die." Mr. Tabby removed his monocle. Then he set a few ivy leaves into the box and replaced the lid. "The examination is concluded," he said. "Good day."

"Good day?" Mrs. Mulberry gasped. "But I didn't get to meet Dr. Woo."

"Indeed you did not." Mr. Tabby jangled his ring of keys.

Ben and Pearl smiled at each other. There'd been no need to worry after all. Mr. Tabby would never let a terrible person like Mrs. Mulberry into the hospital.

Mrs. Mulberry stomped her foot. "But—"

"*But* is a contrary word, madame, and I am in no mood for contrarians today." He grabbed the gate. "Now, if you'd be so kind as to move your red wagon, I shall return to my duties."

Mrs. Mulberry stuck out her chest. "I have duties, too. I'm the president of the Welcome Wagon, and it's *my duty* to meet everyone who moves to Buttonville."

She pointed to the words on her baseball cap: WELCOME WAGON.

As Mr. Tabby tapped his fingers on his key ring, a growl sounded in his throat. Ben could tell, by the peevish look on his face, that he was running out of patience. "Our business is concluded."

Ben didn't want to further annoy Mr. Tabby, but he really wanted to talk about the sickness. After all, if he and Pearl were about to succumb to a strange Imaginary World illness, he'd like to know what to expect. "Mr. Tabby, can I ask you something?" Ben asked. "In private?"

"I have no time today," Mr. Tabby replied. "There are urgent matters to tend to." He attempted to close the gate, but the wagon was still in the way. Victoria's book lay in the wagon's bed.

"I'll help," Pearl said. "Hey, Victoria, move your wagon! Victoria?" Pearl's face suddenly went very pale, and she pointed behind Mr. Tabby.

Victoria Mulberry was at the other end of the driveway, heading straight toward the hospital's open door!

6

EMERGENCY CODE RED

What is that child doing?" Mr. Tabby asked as Victoria barreled up the front stoop, her baseball cap bouncing against her frizzy red hair.

Ben knew exactly what Victoria was doing. She wanted to see the dragon.

"Victoria!" Pearl yelled. "Come back here!"

"Victoria!" Mrs. Mulberry screeched. "Be a good girl and tell Dr. Woo that your mommy wants to meet her!"

"This is an unfortunate turn of events," Mr. Tabby said, shaking his head. "Trespassing can lead to all sorts of unpleasant situations."

"We have to stop her!" Pearl darted around Mr. Tabby and raced up the driveway, gravel crunching beneath her sneakers. Ben had been worried about Mrs. Mulberry getting inside, but it turned out that Victoria was just as sneaky. He squeezed past Mr. Tabby and took off at a full sprint. But before he was even halfway up the driveway, Victoria's red overalls disappeared through the door. Pearl could run like the wind, but she hadn't been fast enough. Victoria was inside!

Ben's mind raced with all sorts of dreadful outcomes. When he'd first visited the hospital, he'd accidentally let the sasquatch escape. The sasquatch had spent the afternoon riding in a grocery cart and eating pudding at the senior center. Thanks to a Sasquatch Catching Kit, the kids had been able to return the big, hairy beast to the hospital before any of Buttonville's residents had noticed. But what if Victoria let something worse escape? Something that made a lot of noise, or had a hankering for flesh instead of pudding? Not every Imaginary creature was as nice as the sasquatch.

Ben pumped his arms as fast as he could. Once he'd dashed up the stairs, he glanced over his shoulder. Somehow, Mr. Tabby had managed to get both Mrs. Mulberry and the red wagon back onto the sidewalk. The gate was closed and padlocked, and Mr. Tabby was hurrying toward the hospital. "Victoria! Be careful!" Mrs. Mulberry yelled.

Ben raced through the doorway. The lobby looked as it always did. The old button factory's sign leaned against the wall, and dusty cobwebs sparkled in the corners of the ceiling. There was a door marked EMPLOYEES ONLY and another marked IDENTIFICATION ROOM. But Victoria was nowhere to be seen.

Ben nearly jumped out of his skin as a siren sounded and a nasal voice blasted from a wall speaker. "Emergency code red, emergency code red. Unauthorized human on the loose. Secure all areas."

Pearl stood at the far end of the lobby, pounding on the closed elevator doors. "Victoria! Come back!"

"I know there's a dragon on the roof," Victoria's muffled voice sounded from inside the elevator. "I want to see it, and you can't stop me!"

Ben leaned over, resting his hands on his knees as he tried to catch his breath. "The elevator doesn't go up that far," he realized. The elevator didn't go to the roof, and it didn't go to the tenth floor, either—which housed the magical Portal, the transportation device that linked the hospital to the Imaginary World. But that was the only good news, because there were eight other floors where Victoria could still get into plenty of trouble.

The elevator hummed. As its panel lit up, the arrow began to drift away from the number one and toward the number two. Victoria was on the move!

"Mr. Tabby!" Pearl cried as he hurried into the lobby. A strand of his long red hair had fallen out of place. "She's in there." Pearl pointed at the elevator.

"Chasing children is *not* part of my job description," Mr. Tabby said grumpily. As the arrow moved past the number two, Mr. Tabby hastily shoved one of his keys into the elevator's panel. The arrow stopped moving. But it had landed on the number three.

"Uh-oh," Ben said.

While Ben and Pearl had never been on the fourth, fifth, sixth, seventh, eighth, or ninth floors of the hospital, they had been to the third floor many times. It was called the Forest Suite because it was a living forest, complete with trees, frogs, and a babbling brook. It was where the sasquatch currently resided while being treated for various ailments like foot fungus and a flea infestation. If Victoria stepped into the Forest Suite, there was no telling what might happen.

"Emergency code red, emergency code red," the nasal voice repeated. "Unauthorized human on the third floor."

Mr. Tabby always kept his cool, even when faced

with situations like percolating pixies and a runaway sasquatch. "I shall take the back stairs. You two will remain here," he told Ben and Pearl.

Pearl groaned. "But—"

Mr. Tabby's response was another growl from deep within his throat. Pearl closed her mouth and nodded. He pressed his palm to the security pad. The EMPLOYEES ONLY door clicked open, and he disappeared, the door closing behind him. Neither Ben nor Pearl had been given security clearance, so they were stuck waiting in the lobby, as instructed.

"He's in an extra-cranky mood today," Ben noted.

"Who can blame him?" Pearl said. "That Victoria makes me so mad! I hope the sasquatch scares the daylights out of her." Pearl paused, then snickered. "I hope it chases her up a tree."

Ben began to pace. Whether or not Victoria got treed was the least of their worries. He felt like a total failure. If he hadn't been distracted by the worm examination, Victoria wouldn't currently be on the third floor, learning all sorts of secrets that could ruin Dr. Woo. He felt kind of sweaty again. Was that from nerves, or the mysterious illness?

"Unauthorized human secured," the nasal voice announced from the speaker. "Emergency code deactivated."

"Woo-hoo!" Pearl cried. "He caught her!"

The elevator made a grinding sound, and the panel lit up again as the elevator descended. Floor two. Floor one. Ben and Pearl waited, both shuffling anxiously as if they had to go to the bathroom. The doors opened.

Mr. Tabby stood inside. A few strands of hair were out of place. He must have run up the back staircase. He held tightly to Victoria's arm. She looked mostly the same—her frizzy hair, her thick glasses perched on her nose. Except she was as pale as the moon.

"B...b...b..." Victoria mumbled as Mr. Tabby led her into the lobby. "B...b...b..."

"She looks scared," Ben whispered to Pearl.

"She looks weird," Pearl said. "What's the matter with her face?" Under normal circumstances, that particular question would be considered rude. But Victoria *did* look weird. Not only had her face turned as pale as the moon, but it was almost as round as well. And getting rounder by the second.

"B...b...b..." Victoria stammered. Her neck began to swell.

"Ewww. What's wrong with her?" Pearl asked.

"I shall explain momentarily," Mr. Tabby said. "In the meantime, I will escort her back to her mother." Keeping a firm grip on Victoria's arm, he led her outside. Ben and Pearl followed down the long driveway.

Mrs. Mulberry was waiting behind the gate. "What happened?" she called. "Did you meet Dr. Woo? What's she like? Tell me everything!"

Mr. Tabby unlocked the gate and gently, but insistently, pushed Victoria onto the sidewalk, next to her mother. Mrs. Mulberry shrieked. "What the matter with my baby? What's the matter with her *face*?"

After smoothing a few wrinkles from his vest, Mr. Tabby looked at Mrs. Mulberry with a sneer

of disapproval. "Your daughter was trespassing. Trespassing can lead to all sorts of *unpleasant* outcomes."

"Unpleasant?" Mrs. Mulberry jabbed a finger at Mr. Tabby. "Why is her head so round? I demand an explanation!"

Ben shuffled nervously, wondering what sort of story Mr. Tabby would come up with. The assistant cleared his throat and stood very straight. He stared down his nose and spoke in a calm manner, as if having one's head expand was nothing to worry about. "It would appear that your daughter is ill. I suggest you take her home and put her to bed."

"B...b...big," Victoria said, finally forming a word. "F...f...furry."

Ben cringed. *Big* and *furry* could only mean one thing. She'd seen the sasquatch. But what was happening to her? Both he and Pearl gasped and took a step back as Victoria's neck got even bigger. Victoria tried to talk, but no more words came out. Ben couldn't believe what he was seeing. Even after everything he'd been exposed to at Dr. Woo's hospital and in the Imaginary World, Victoria's swollen head was the weirdest yet.

"She's blowing up like a balloon!" Mrs. Mulberry cried.

"The swelling is most unfortunate." Mr. Tabby's pupils flashed. "However, all good things must come to an end. Our business is now concluded."

"We'd better get you to the doctor," Mrs. Mulberry said. "The *real* doctor, not some fake worm doctor." She pushed Victoria into the red wagon, then began pulling it up the street toward town.

"Good day," Mr. Tabby said with a wave of his hand.

"Something happened inside your hospital!" Mrs. Mulberry yelled over her shoulder. "And as soon as Victoria's face deflates, I'm going to find out what!"

Once the Mulberrys were out of earshot, Pearl broke into a string of questions. "Did she see the sasquatch? Did it chase her up a tree? What will happen if she tells everyone? How come her face looks like that? Will she be that way forever? She was the Princess of Buttons in last year's parade, and I

don't think she can be princess again if her head is as big as a balloon. What do you think?"

Mr. Tabby held up a hand to silence Pearl. Both she and Ben were quiet, waiting for his answer. "Whether or not Victoria is a princess in a parade is the least of our worries," he replied. "There is another matter to which we must attend. For when that human child stepped out of the elevator and into the Forest Suite, she entered an area that is currently under quarantine."

"Quarantine?" Ben's stomach tightened. "That means it's off limits because someone is sick. Is the sasquatch sick? Does it have the same thing that Dr. Woo has? Is it bad?"

Mr. Tabby nodded. "The sasquatch and Dr. Woo are both ill with Troll Tonsillitis. Your acquaintance is showing early symptoms. Unfortunately, the infection is not only unpleasant, it is also highly contagious." The next thing he said made Ben shudder. "I predict that Troll Tonsillitis will spread throughout Buttonville in a matter of hours."

7

TROLL TONSILLITIS

"Troll Tonsillitis?" Pearl furrowed her brow. "I didn't know trolls had tonsils. Well, actually, I don't know anything about trolls."

Ben put a hand to his throat. "Is it anything like regular tonsillitis? I had that a lot when I was little."

"Me too," Pearl said.

Mr. Tabby explained, "While the human version of tonsillitis is not contagious, the troll version spreads with the inhalation of a single stray germ. The victim's face and neck puff up, giving the individual a troll-like appearance. Trolls are not *attractive* creatures."

Ben had never seen a troll, but Victoria had certainly looked gruesome.

"Is Victoria's head going to explode?" Pearl asked. "I may not like her very much, but I wouldn't want anyone's head to explode. That would be terrible."

"There will be no exploding," Mr. Tabby said. "But she will not return to normal unless we administer the proper medication. Nor will Dr. Woo or the sasquatch."

Ben suddenly remembered something very important. "Metalmouth is sick, too!"

"Oh dear." Mr. Tabby made a *tsk-tsk* sound. "This shall prove most difficult. Dragons do not like taking medicine."

"He sneezed all over us," Ben added. "We definitely inhaled some of those germs."

Mr. Tabby looked worriedly at Ben, then at Pearl. "Do either of you possess tonsils?"

"I had to go to the hospital and get mine taken out," Ben said.

"Me too. See." Pearl opened her mouth real wide as evidence. Ben stood on tiptoe and peeked past her molars. Sure enough, no tonsils. Along with being Dr. Woo's apprentices and sharing all sorts of secrets, this was another amazing thing he and Pearl had in common.

"If you do not possess tonsils, then you will not catch Troll Tonsillitis," Mr. Tabby said. Ben sighed with relief. That was excellent news. Mr. Tabby continued. "I do not possess them, either. So it would appear that we three will escape the epidemic."

"Poor Dr. Woo," Pearl said with a frown. "I don't want her to look like a troll."

Ben agreed. Even with the scars that ran across her cheek and her neck, Dr. Woo was one of the prettiest people he'd ever known. He couldn't imagine her with a puffy face and a thick troll neck. Even though the sasquatch wasn't *attractive*, except maybe to another sasquatch, Ben had spent enough time with the furry beast to care about its well-being. And Metalmouth was his friend, so of course he didn't want the dragon to be sick. "What about Dr. Woo's special soup?" Ben asked. Last week, both he and Pearl had caught a cold from a leprechaun, and the soup had instantly cured them. "Won't that work?"

"The special soup has no effect on Troll Tonsillitis,"

Mr. Tabby said. "The only cure is ground griffin feather."

"What's a griffin?" Pearl asked.

Ben knew this answer because the emblem on one of his father's fancy cars was a griffin. "It's a beast that's half eagle and half lion."

Mr. Tabby raised his eyebrows as if impressed by Ben's level of knowledge. "That is correct. Unfortunately, after an extensive search of Dr. Woo's medicine cabinet, I have found not a single speck of ground griffin feather." He pulled a pocket watch from his vest. "I must make haste. It is time for me to check the doctor's temperature." He ushered them onto the sidewalk.

"You want us to leave?" Pearl asked. "But aren't we going to help you?"

"Today is Tuesday. You do not apprentice on Tuesday."

"But what about tomorrow?" Ben said. "Is our apprenticeship still canceled?"

"Hmmm. I must think about that for a moment."

Mr. Tabby tapped a finger to his chin. "Seeing as you do not possess tonsils and are, therefore, not in danger of catching Troll Tonsillitis, I am uncanceling."

"Yay!" Pearl shouted.

Ben was also excited, though he couldn't help but imagine his grandfather and the other seniors with big balloon heads. It would be pretty difficult to play board games at the senior center if everyone kept tipping over. "What are we going to do if there's no griffin feather?"

"We shall have to get one," Mr. Tabby said.

"Did you say *we*? You mean *we're* going to the Imaginary World?" Pearl started bouncing on her toes. "Seriously? You, me, and Ben? All three of us?"

Ben chewed on his lower lip. Another trip to the Imaginary World? Perhaps they'd misheard Mr. Tabby. Maybe he'd mixed up his pronouns, saying *we* by accident. Pearl kept bouncing, as if the sidewalk were made of rubber. Ben, however, stood perfectly still.

Mr. Tabby released a long, exasperated sigh. "It distresses me greatly to admit that I cannot accomplish this task on my own." He closed the gate, then locked it. With the key ring dangling from his long fingertips, he began to walk back up the driveway, toward the hospital.

Ben and Pearl watched from the other side of the gate. Was that it? "Mr. Tabby?" Ben called. "What are we supposed to do in the meantime? What if people start getting sick?"

Mr. Tabby didn't answer those questions. "Arrive tomorrow at eight thirty AM precisely," he said over his shoulder. "And wear your fanciest clothes. One must always look nice when meeting a griffin."

8

TROLLVILLE

Ben and Pearl hurried down Fir Street, heading into town. "I can hardly wait for tomorrow," Pearl said, her ponytail bouncing. "I *love* going to the Imaginary World."

"Me too," Ben mumbled, because only half of him was excited. The other half, mostly his stomach, was filled with flutters, as if a butterfly had been swallowed and trapped.

"Why do you have that weird look on your face?" Pearl asked. "Are you worried?"

"No," Ben said. He didn't want Pearl to think he was scared. Meeting a half-lion, half-eagle creature would be totally cool, of course. It was the *getting there* that made him nervous. Traveling to another dimension was fraught with all sorts of dangers, such as the possibility of falling between dimensions and getting lost forever! But Pearl didn't seem to fret about stuff like that.

There was another danger—the possibility of coming face-to-face with a certain bad guy named Maximus Steele, a poacher who'd somehow gotten himself into the Imaginary World. He'd stolen the rain dragon's horn and had tried to trap a unicorn foal. He was pure evil, and Ben didn't want to run into him.

"Why do you think we have to wear our fanciest clothes?" Pearl asked. "I don't have anything fancy." To Ben, this statement seemed true because Pearl wore the same thing every day—a pair of basketball shorts, a plain T-shirt, and sneakers. He'd never seen her in a dress, tights, or jewelry. She did,

however, own a pair of magical pink shoes, given to her by the same leprechaun who'd given them each a cold. "Oh, wait, I have one skirt. Mom made me wear it to my cousin's wedding. I hate it, but I'll wear it if it means I get to go to the Imaginary World again."

Ben was used to nice clothes. His mom ordered from all the trendiest catalogs. Before he'd left for Buttonville, she'd packed him a suit, just in case something special came up. She'd probably imagined a town picnic or a block party—not a meeting with *a griffin.*

Ben and Pearl took a right turn onto Main Street. Although Buttonville didn't have the excitement of a big city, it did have its small charms. Like a diner that made the entire town smell like hamburgers and a cinema that played old black-and-white movies. And the colorful buttons that could be found here and there, blown by wind and collected by pigeons—like little pieces of treasure.

"Hello, Ms. Nod," Pearl said. Ms. Nod, the owner

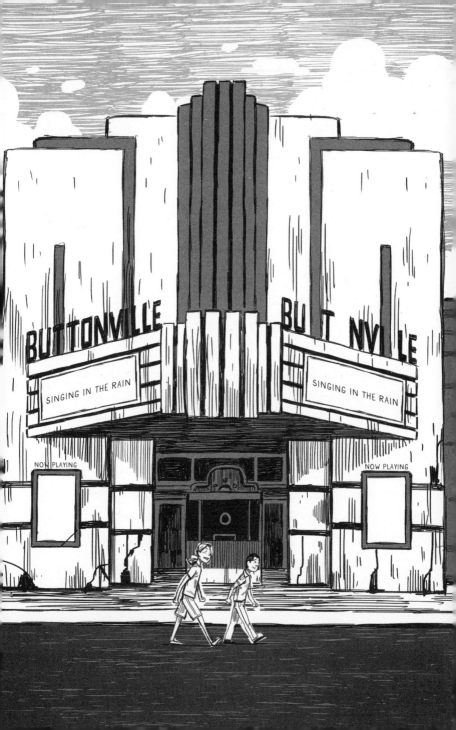

of the Buttonville Bookstore, was taping a CLOSED sign to its door. "How come you're closing in the middle of the day?" When Ms. Nod turned around, both Ben and Pearl discovered the reason.

Beneath her red-framed glasses, her face was all puffy and much rounder than usual.

"Uh-oh," Ben said. Right before their eyes, her neck began to swell. Ben didn't mean to stare, but it was like watching a bullfrog puff out its face.

"S...s...sick," she whispered. Then, purse in hand, she hurried away, teetering beneath her oversize head.

"I'm so glad I don't have tonsils," Pearl said. "But how'd Ms. Nod catch Troll Tonsillitis already?"

Ben looked around. "Mrs. Mulberry and Victoria must have walked past the bookstore. Or maybe the wind blew Metalmouth's germs onto Main Street." It only took *one* germ, according to Mr. Tabby. "Mr. Tabby's right. It's going to spread all over." If everyone started to look like trolls, would Buttonville become Trollville?

"I sure hope my parents don't have tonsils," Pearl

said as she pushed open the Dollar Store door. "Well, I gotta unpack boxes. See you tomorrow. It's gonna be great!" She waved good-bye.

"I hope you're right." *Great* would be way better than *dangerous*.

Ben darted past a couple more people with bloated faces. A woman shrieked when she spied her reflection in a store window. "What's happening?" she cried.

Ben might have stopped to explain the situation, but that would have meant breaking the contract of secrecy he and Pearl had signed. "I don't know," he told her, then quickened his pace.

Even if the journey to the Imaginary World was riddled with danger, Ben knew he couldn't chicken out. Dr. Woo, the sasquatch, Metalmouth, and all the sick residents of Buttonville needed a special feather. And he and Pearl were going to get it.

But why did they have to dress up?

9

PLAYING DRESS-UP

The next day, Ben's grandfather dropped Ben off at Dr. Woo's Worm Hospital at 8:18 AM, a little early because he wanted to get to the Food 4 Less Market to buy more matzo ball mix. Word of the mysterious epidemic was spreading as fast as the disease itself. "Give this soup to Dr. Woo to keep her healthy," Grandpa Abe said, handing Ben a small plaid thermos. "Tell her it's an old family recipe. I'll send more as soon as I make it." Luckily, Grandpa Abe's tonsils had been removed sometime during the last century, so he'd woken up with a normal-sized head.

Ben didn't have the heart to tell his grandfather that matzo ball soup wouldn't help the doctor. It might taste delicious, but it couldn't cure a disease from the Imaginary World.

When Pearl arrived at the hospital gate at 8:22 AM, Ben almost didn't recognize her. Her long blond hair hung loose, and she'd tied an oversize yellow bow to the top of her head. Ben thought this made her look like a birthday present.

"Don't say anything about my skirt," she told him with a roll of her eyes. "I already know it looks like a lace factory exploded all over me." Then she smiled slyly. "I'm wearing my basketball shorts underneath. I want to be comfortable, don't I?"

Ben wasn't comfortable. He was sweating something fierce. His shirt was buttoned all the way to his chin, and his tie felt like a noose. He'd completed the outfit with a pair of pressed pants and brand-new, stiff black dress shoes.

"This might be the most important trip we take

to the Imaginary World," Pearl said as she fiddled with her bow. "Both my mom and dad woke up with Troll Tonsillitis. Their faces are so round they look like Mr. and Mrs. Potato Head. There's already a long line in front of the doctor's office, but what's he going to do? He doesn't have a griffin feather."

Ben thought it was odd that Buttonville had only one doctor for people. There were doctors all over Los Angeles—five in his neighborhood alone. If you strained your elbow during a tennis game, you could see a sports-injury doctor. If you got a sunburn at the beach, you could go to a skin doctor. And if you wanted to freeze your face so you didn't have any wrinkles, you had your choice of about a zillion plastic surgeons. "Don't worry," Ben said. "We'll get a feather, and then your parents will be back to normal."

At precisely 8:30, Mr. Tabby opened the gate and led them toward the hospital. He looked particularly dashing in a metallic gold vest. "Are we fancy enough?" Pearl asked.

"It would appear that you actually *followed* my

instructions," Mr. Tabby replied with an approving nod. "Well done."

Ben smiled. It was rare to get a compliment from Mr. Tabby.

As they walked, Pearl launched a round of questions. "How long will it take to get there? Does the griffin live in the mountains or in a forest? Does it eat lion food or eagle food? Is it old? Do its babies hatch from eggs or are they born? Where does it—?"

"Questions are cheap and easy to find," Mr. Tabby interrupted, his voice stern. "Answers are like treasures, waiting to be revealed."

"Huh?" Pearl scrunched up her face. Then she shrugged.

As soon as they were inside, Ben closed the hospital's front door and slid the five dead bolts in place. The bolts had been installed to provide extra security against anyone who might want to sneak into Dr. Woo's hospital and uncover secrets—or worse, steal them!

"My grandpa sent some soup for Dr. Woo, to keep her healthy," Ben said, holding out the thermos.

"I didn't tell him she was already sick." Ben hoped Dr. Woo wasn't feeling too bad with her face and neck all puffed up like a blowfish. "There's enough soup for the sasquatch, too, but I'm not sure if there's enough for Metalmouth." Ben guessed that two or three gallons of soup would be considered a single serving for a dragon.

Mr. Tabby took the thermos. "That was considerate." He set it aside in the Identification Room. "But right now there is no time for soup consumption or dillydallying of any sort. We must prepare for our journey."

Mr. Tabby led them through the EMPLOYEES ONLY door. Because this was Ben's and Pearl's fourth official visit as apprentices, they knew exactly what to do. They punched their time cards at the clock, then thumbtacked them to the ON DUTY side of the bulletin board. That's when Ben noticed something was different. "How come Violet's card is on the off-duty side?" he asked. Violet was the switchboard operator who worked on the tenth floor, fielding emergency calls

from the Imaginary World. She was a satyress—half human, half goat.

"I'm afraid Violet is also ill with Troll Tonsillitis. Her brother is working in her stead."

Sure enough, a card belonging to Vinny was tacked to the ON DUTY side. Neither Ben nor Pearl had met Vinny. "If he's Violet's brother, then is he half goat, too?" Pearl asked.

Mr. Tabby flared his nostrils. "Vinny is a satyr, not a goat. Do try to use the correct terminology."

"Wow," Pearl whispered to Ben. "We get to meet a half man, half goat *and* a half lion, half eagle."

While that seemed like an amazing opportunity, an important question popped into Ben's head. "Uh, Mr. Tabby? What number does the griffin get on the danger scale?" The danger scale was a measurement used to rate an Imaginary creature. The number one was given to the least dangerous, like a gentle unicorn foal, and the number five-plus went to the most dangerous, like a child-eating kelpie. "I just want to be prepared," Ben added, so Pearl wouldn't

think he was scared. "In case it rates a five-plus."

"Firstly, let me make it perfectly clear that the griffin is not an *it*. He is a *he*. And secondly, though he possesses talons, claws, *and* a razor-sharp beak, his mood determines his danger rating," Mr. Tabby explained. "Let us hope he is in a good mood, and let us do our best not to annoy him."

Ben and Mr. Tabby looked directly at Pearl. "Why's everyone staring at me?" she said. "I won't annoy the griffin. Well, not on purpose."

"Maybe go easy on the questions," Ben said gently. He didn't want to hurt her feelings, but she did tend to ask a lot of questions.

Pearl scowled and was about to say something, when Mr. Tabby cleared his throat, as if preparing for a speech. "I am about to deliver important instructions, so I require your full attention."

"Okay," Ben said. "I'm listening."

Pearl scratched beneath her yellow ribbon. "Me too."

Mr. Tabby pressed his fingertips together. "There is only one way to get a griffin's feather. It must be

given by the griffin himself. He is protective of his feathers and will only grant one if someone has made him happy. The best way to make a griffin happy is to engage in a battle of riddles. Are either of you skilled in the art of riddling?"

"I know some knock-knock jokes," Pearl said. "Knock, knock." She pointed at Mr. Tabby. "You're supposed to say, who's there?"

"Jokes are not the same as riddles," Mr. Tabby said, his gold vest shimmering beneath the hallway's lights. "A joke has a punch line. A riddle is a story with an answer."

"Oh. Well, then Ben can tell the riddles because he's super good at making up stories." Pearl nudged Ben with her elbow.

"I guess so," Ben said.

"That is excellent news." Mr. Tabby nodded approvingly, then continued with the instructions. "In addition to our fancy clothing, our manners during our visit must be fancy as well. Do either of you know how to bow?"

"Sure," Pearl said. "I bow at my piano recitals."

She leaned so far forward it looked like she was preparing for a somersault.

Mr. Tabby returned her to an upright position. "Allow me to demonstrate the correct form." He placed one arm behind his back and swept the other arm through the air, bowing at the waist until he was at a perfect ninety-degree angle. Then he straightened. "Your turn." It took Ben and Pearl three tries each before Mr. Tabby nodded and said, "Not perfect but acceptable."

"Why are we bowing?" Ben asked.

"One must always bow in the presence of royalty."

"Royalty?" Pearl said the word so loudly it echoed down the hall. She pushed the big, drooping ribbon out of her eyes. "Are we going to see the unicorn princess again? Or the unicorn king?"

Mr. Tabby grabbed a black satchel from the supply closet. "I doubt we will encounter a unicorn. They rarely leave the Tangled Forest, and our journey will take us to the center of the Imaginary World."

"Then what royalty are we meeting?" Ben asked.

Mr. Tabby's mustache twitched. "The griffin king, of course. Have you not been paying attention?"

"The griffin is a *king*?" Pearl asked.

"He is not *a* king. He is *the* king. The griffin is king of the *entire* Imaginary World." Mr. Tabby's yellow eyes flashed. "And that is why you must remember my instructions. Because if he becomes displeased, the griffin king has the power to keep us in his world forever."

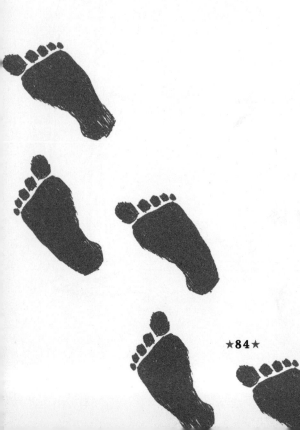

10

Keep us in his world *forever*?" Ben asked, his voice cracking.

Mr. Tabby closed the supply closet door. "The griffin king can do whatever he likes. It is possible he is the reason why our last apprentice never returned." Without further explanation, Mr. Tabby headed down the hallway, black satchel in hand.

Ben didn't follow. He was trying to process what he'd just heard.

During their first official day as apprentices, Mr. Tabby had told them that punching in and punching out at the time clock was required. The previous apprentice had forgotten to clock in and out, and now no one knew whether she was in the Known World or in the Imaginary World. She'd *mysteriously* disappeared.

"Come on," Pearl urged, pulling on his sleeve. "We can't get any answers if we just stand here all day."

As usual, Pearl went first. It wasn't that Ben was a coward, but Pearl tended to face things head-on, while Ben liked to mull things over. His mother called him "cautious." Thanks to his visit with the rain dragon, Ben now understood that he and Pearl were opposites, like yin and yang. That was why they made good partners. His common sense tamed her wild streak. Her boldness pushed him to try new things.

But his common sense was screaming at him. *Don't go! Make up a story! Stay here!*

Then he remembered that Dr. Woo, the sasquatch, Metalmouth, Violet, Pearl's parents, Ms. Nod, Victoria, and a lot of other Buttonville residents were sick. So he followed.

In order to get to the Imaginary World, Mr. Tabby, Ben, and Pearl needed to catch a ride in the Portal, which was located on the tenth floor. For security reasons, the only access was through the back stairwell. While Ben struggled to keep up with Mr. Tabby's quick pace, Pearl bounded up the stairs like a jackrabbit. "I've only met one real king, and he was a unicorn. Does the griffin king wear a crown? Does he have a castle? What about a throne? Can I sit on it? Do we call him Your Majesty, or Your Highness, or Mr. King?"

Mr. Tabby ignored Pearl's questions, as he often did. And he said nothing more about the missing apprentice. When they reached the tenth-floor landing, a sign greeted them.

Mr. Tabby wrapped his long fingers around the doorknob.

"Wait…" Ben said. He loosened his tie, then bent over, hands on his knees, trying to catch his breath. "Shouldn't we talk about this? I mean, aren't you going to tell us about the other apprentice?"

"There is nothing more to tell," Mr. Tabby said. "She was here and then she wasn't."

"But where'd she go?" Ben asked. "Why didn't she come back?"

Pearl bent over so she and Ben were face-to-face. "Don't worry. We'll come back, I promise. There's no way the griffin king will keep us. If he tries, I'll ask him a million questions. It'll drive him crazy. He'll beg us to leave!"

Ben nodded. That actually sounded like a good plan.

"Have you finished with your *discussion*?" Mr. Tabby asked. Ben and Pearl straightened and gave him their full attention. "In a moment you shall meet Vinny, Violet's brother. Vinny is not like Violet. He lacks charm. He lacks finesse. Do not speak to him unless it is absolutely necessary. And whatever you do, do not, I repeat, *do not* turn your back to him."

"Why?" Pearl asked.

"*Y* is a letter in the alphabet," Mr. Tabby told her. Then he opened the door.

A vast room spread before them. Yellow fairy dust covered the floor. Because the dust had already been used to power the Portal, all its magic had been drained, so no one bothered to sweep it up. Walking through it was like walking through spilled glitter.

The room was mostly empty, except for an enormous switchboard that covered the far wall. Though it looked like old-fashioned technology, the switchboard was a complex contraption, providing a way to talk to the Imaginary World. Violet usually sat on the operator's stool, in a colorful dress with matching high heels and a beehive hairdo that looked like vanilla soft-serve. She always greeted the apprentices with a friendly "Howdy, y'aaaaall."

The satyr who sat on the stool now was twice as big as Violet and dressed in blue pajamas. His face was goatlike, with small eyes, a bushy beard, and little goat ears. Furry legs poked out from the bottom of his pajama pants, and his feet were actually hooves.

"Good day, Vinny," Mr. Tabby said.

Vinny reached into a bag of oats. "What's good about it? My sister went and got herself sick with Troll Tonsillitis, so now I gotta work the day shift. I hate the day shift. I'm supposed to be sleeeeeping." He stuffed his mouth, chewed, and stared at Ben and Pearl in a brooding way. "Whatcha looking aaaaat?"

"Nothing," Ben lied.

"We weren't looking at you, that's for sure," Pearl said. But neither she nor Ben could peel their gazes from the sharp horns that jutted out of Vinny's black hair. Violet didn't have horns.

Vinny ate more oats. "These the new apprentices? Whooeeh, they got themselves some fancy duuuuuds."

"There is no time for formal introductions," Mr. Tabby said. "We must make haste. The apprentices and I are heading to the griffin's palace."

"Going to see the king, are ya?" Vinny wiped his mouth with his pajama sleeve. "I've never met the king. Guess I'm not *fancy* enough."

"One must dress appropriately when meeting royalty," Mr. Tabby told him. "Now, if you would be so kind as to—"

"Hold on a cotton-picking minute." Vinny tossed the bag of oats aside and stood. He was twice as tall as Ben had expected. "I thought you wasn't supposed to go through the Portal. Says so right theeeeere." He pointed to a note taped to the switchboard. Ben had never noticed it before.

Until further notice, Mr. Tabby is forbidden access to the Imaginary World.
—Dr. Woo

Ben looked at Pearl and mouthed the word *forbidden*. Pearl shrugged.

Mr. Tabby reached into his vest pocket and pulled out a note. "Dr. Woo has made an exception in this case and has authorized my journey."

Vinny grabbed the paper, glancing at it. "How do I know this is reeeeeal?"

Mr. Tabby growled softly. His irises flashed as if they'd suddenly caught fire. "Are you questioning my honesty?"

"Maybe I is and maybe I ain't." Vinny snorted. Then he ate Dr. Woo's note. "Why would you want to go back in there anyways? Don't you remember what happened last time you weeeeent?"

"It was an unfortunate incident," Mr. Tabby said. "However, this time I am taking precautions." He patted the black satchel. "Now, my good fellow, it is imperative that we take this journey. Troll Tonsillitis is spreading quickly. You would like us to cure your sister, would you not?"

"Sure I want you to cure her. I don't want to get stuck working another day shift."

"Then be so kind as to summon the Portal."

A shiver—part excitement, part dread—trickled up Ben's legs. The Portal's arrival was a sight to behold. He turned around, expecting to hear sounds of distant thunder.

Whunk!

Ben sailed through the air, landing in the center of the room. Fairy-dust clouds formed on either side of him, then settled back to the floor. "Ouch," he cried, rubbing his bottom. "What happened?" Pearl ran backward until she reached him. She helped him to his feet so that they were both facing the switchboard.

"You turned around," she whispered. "Mr. Tabby warned us to not turn our backs on Vinny. He butted you with his horns." She giggled. "Sorry, but it was kinda funny."

Ben had to think about this for a moment. Vinny was half goat, and goats were known to ram things with their horns. But it *wasn't* funny.

Vinny didn't apologize. He returned to his stool without a word, acting as if head-butting a person in

the rump was a perfectly normal thing to do. Then he pressed a big yellow button.

Thunder sounded in the distance as if a natural disaster were rolling toward the hospital. A wisp appeared in the center of the tenth floor, hovering in the air. As it began to rotate, it formed a baby tornado, growing larger and larger until it touched the ground and the ceiling. Gusts blew across Ben's face and through his hair. Fairy dust was swept up, turning the churning vortex lemon yellow.

"Now!" Mr. Tabby hollered above the wind. The black satchel in hand, he ran directly at the tornado and disappeared inside. Pearl didn't hesitate. As she raced into the Portal, her skirt blew straight up, revealing her basketball shorts. The wind stung Ben's face and shrieked in his ears. He glanced at Vinny, who'd grabbed the bag and was stuffing oats into his mouth.

"Hey, kid, you want my advice?" Oats tumbled onto his beard. "You'd better practice saying, 'Here, kitty, kitty, kitty.'"

"Why?" Ben asked.

"You'll find out sooooon enough." Then Vinny belly-laughed so hard the bag of oats tumbled off his lap.

Ben decided right then and there that he didn't like Vinny. The satyr was loud and rude, and there was that whole head-butting thing. Hopefully, once Violet was cured, Vinny could go back to the night shift, and Ben and Pearl wouldn't have to deal with him again.

Lightning zapped, turning the tornado bright white. Ben squeezed his eyes shut and ran straight into the wind.

11

CAT MAN

Asingle bulb flicked on above Ben's head. He stood inside the Portal's inner chamber, a space that was quiet and calm. While the floor was solid, the walls were formed by the vortex swirling around the perimeter. Ben would have felt a lot more secure if the walls had been made of plywood instead of wind. A person can't tumble backward and fall through wood.

"Destination, please?" The squeaky voice belonged

to the Portal's captain, someone the apprentices had never met. While they'd always heard his voice, they'd never seen him. And since there was no place for the captain to hide, Ben was starting to believe that the captain wasn't actually on board the Portal. Instead, his voice was being transmitted from someplace else. Maybe a control tower. Ben wondered what kind of a creature he was.

"The griffin's palace," Mr. Tabby said.

"Oooh, a palace," Pearl whispered to Ben.

"Setting course coordinates," the pilot announced. "Fasten your seat belts and prepare for takeoff." But there were no belts, because there were no seats. Dr. Woo had said they were being reupholstered. Ben thought this was very strange, *and* very dangerous. Seat belts were the law back home.

The floor began to vibrate. Ben stepped closer to Pearl, keeping as far away from the edges as possible. He didn't want to admit that he'd had a couple of nightmares about falling out and finding himself all alone in the middle of nowhere.

After informing the pilot of their destination, Mr. Tabby remained silent, both hands clutching his satchel.

The trip lasted a good five minutes, which was a very long time to be jostled about. "I could never be an astronaut," Pearl said as she held both hands over her stomach. "Why is this taking so long? Can't this thing go any faster?"

Ben had no idea how fast they were going. Thanks to his math teacher, who'd taught a unit on speed, Ben knew that airplanes flying between Los Angeles and Buttonville travel at roughly 460 miles per hour. He'd learned that sound travels at around 700 miles per hour and that light travels at 186,000 miles per second. In science-fiction movies, starships dart between galaxies at warp speed. But how fast did one travel between dimensions? According to the training video he and Pearl had watched, the Portal moved in all directions at once. But if you moved in all directions at once, didn't that mean you weren't moving at all?

"Are we there yet?" Pearl asked.

"Destination ahead. Prepare for landing," the pilot said.

Ben wasn't sure what to do, so he stiffened his legs and gripped the soles of his shoes with his toes. Just as his stomach began to churn, the turbulence stopped. "Destination reached," the pilot announced. An EXIT sign illuminated. "Thank you for choosing the Portal for your interdimensional travel needs."

"Finally," Pearl said, followed by a little burp. "I thought I was going to lose my breakfast."

Ben unclenched his jaw and sighed with relief. They'd made the journey in one piece. There was, of course, still a return trip to worry about. He wouldn't feel completely at ease until he'd touched down on the tenth floor and could feel the dust-covered floorboards beneath his shoes.

"Mr. Tabby?" Pearl asked. "What's wrong?"

Mr. Tabby stood perfectly still, staring at the EXIT sign.

"Mr. Tabby?" Pearl gently tapped on his arm. "Shouldn't we go?"

He didn't move. He didn't even blink. What was he thinking? Was he worried about something?

"Mr. Tabby?" Ben said quietly. Did he dare ask the question? "Why did the note say you were *forbidden access* to the Imaginary World?" He and Pearl waited, their anxious breathing the only sound within the Portal. Even the mysterious pilot, who usually told them to make their way to the exit, was quiet.

Mr. Tabby took a long, deep breath. Then he set the satchel on the floor and looked at the apprentices. "Before we step into the Imaginary World, there is something I must tell you." He tugged on his vest, smoothing out a few wrinkles. "I am not *exactly* as I seem."

Ben pondered this statement. Couldn't he say the same thing about himself? Everyone might think he looked like an ordinary boy. But he'd traveled between dimensions, played fetch with a dragon, and been head-butted by a satyr. There was nothing ordinary about that.

"I know why you're not exactly as you seem," Pearl said to Mr. Tabby. "You're a cat. I figured that out a long time ago."

Ben winced, expecting Mr. Tabby to growl with disapproval. Sure, Ben had the same suspicions, but he wasn't going to come right out and accuse Dr. Woo's assistant of being a cat. That seemed kind of rude.

But the evidence did add up. When Ben met Mr. Tabby for the first time, he'd made a comment about hamsters tasting delicious with pepper. Another time, he'd mentioned that parakeets tasted good with mustard. Then there was the way he growled, the way his yellow eyes flashed, and his amazing sense of smell. And who could ignore that mustache? It looked just like a set of whiskers.

There'd also been a tail. Both Ben and Pearl had seen it. Just one time, though.

"Is it true?" Ben asked.

"Of course it's true," Pearl said. "He eats those furry mouse crackers."

"Mackers," Mr. Tabby corrected. He opened the satchel and pulled out a box.

MACKERS
MOUSE-FLAVORED CRACKERS
YOU'D HAVE TO BE WACKERS TO EAT ONLY ONE.

"I suggest you put a few in your pockets," he advised. "I cannot resist the odor of mouse, and you may need to tempt me from wandering."

"Wandering?" Ben asked as he grabbed a couple of crackers by their tails and tucked them in his pocket.

"When I'm transformed into my feline shape, my

instincts take over. I cannot resist the scent of mouse, or rat, or any rodent-type creature."

"Transformed?" Pearl bounced on her toes. "You mean I'm right? You're a cat?"

"I am a bakeneko," he said. "A shape-shifting cat. I was born in the Imaginary World, so my true form is feline. But when I live in the Known World, I take on the form of Mr. Tabby. I must have opposable thumbs in order to do my job as Dr. Woo's assistant."

"Cool," Ben said. "But if you were born in the Imaginary World, then why did Vinny show us that note, saying you were forbidden to come here?"

"The moment I step into the Imaginary World, I return to my bakeneko shape. And the longer I stay in this world, the more catlike I become. If I stay too long, I will forget all about my life with Dr. Woo."

"Oh, that would be bad," Pearl said. "Then you shouldn't leave the Portal. We can get the griffin's feather by ourselves. All we need are directions to the palace."

"Directions won't suffice. And no map exists," Mr. Tabby said. "Only those who have been before can find the griffin's palace. That is why I have accompanied you today." He pulled a harness and leash from the satchel. "When we step into the Imaginary World, you must immediately place this around me. Never let me off the leash or out of your sight." He looked at them sternly. "Do not let me wander. And if the mission should go awry, do not leave me behind. Do you understand?"

"We'd never leave you behind," Pearl said, grabbing the leash and harness. Ben nodded in agreement.

Mr. Tabby reached into the satchel again and removed a vial of yellow fairy dust that hung on a string. He slipped it around his neck. The dust was their only way to summon the Portal for the return trip. "I will lead you to the palace, but I will not be able to speak. It will be up to you to get the feather from the griffin king. Remember to bow and to be very polite. Dr. Woo is counting on you. Are you ready?"

"Of course," Pearl said. "This won't be too hard. You lead us to the king, and we ask him for a feather. What could go wrong?"

Ben almost laughed. If there was one thing he knew for certain, something *always* went wrong. But then again, something always went right, too.

Leaving the satchel behind, Mr. Tabby stepped beneath the EXIT sign, into the swirling wind, and disappeared from view. Pearl gave Ben a reassuring smile, then followed. Ben hesitated. Was Mr. Tabby really going to turn into a cat? Would the griffin king like them enough to give them a feather? Would they find out what had happened to the last apprentice?

And the biggest worry of all—would they run into the dangerous Maximus Steele?

"Proceed to the exit," the pilot ordered.

The wind whipped Ben's hair and howled in his ears as he pushed through the tornado. As soon as he stepped into the Imaginary World, the Portal vanished. No wind. No thunder. Just silence.

Except for a quiet little sound, like a miniature motorboat engine.

Ben looked down.

Sitting at his feet was a reddish-orange cat with big yellow eyes and twitching whiskers.

And he was purring.

12

AN AMAZING MAZE

O h, he's sooooo cute," Pearl said with a happy
squeal. She dropped the harness and leash.
Then she wrapped her arms around the cat's
belly and lifted him.

"*Eroooow*," the cat complained, his legs dangling.
Ben thought this was very embarrassing. The cat
might look like an ordinary cat, but he was still
Mr. Tabby, wasn't he? And Pearl was treating him
like a stuffed animal. The whole thing was very
weird.

The cat began to squirm, slipping from Pearl's grip. "Uh-oh," she said. "He's trying to get away."

Ben grabbed the harness and quickly fastened it around the cat's middle. "Sorry," he said. "But I'm just following your orders." Once the harness was secure, Ben attached the leash. His hand brushed against the little vial of fairy dust that hung around the cat's neck. "We should take care of the vial," Ben told Pearl. "It's our only way back."

"Right," Pearl said. She reached for it.

Ben had never seen a cat throw such a fit. He hissed and spat. His hair stood on end as if he'd been caught in an electrical storm. He swung both front paws at Ben. "Ow!" Ben cried, stepping back as three red welts rose on his hand. "He scratched me!" As the cat aimed at Pearl, she dropped him. He landed on all fours, as cats tend to do. Then he tried to shake free of the harness and leash. When that didn't work, he hissed at Pearl, hissed at Ben, then sat and proceeded to clean a front paw.

"Guess he wants to keep the vial," Ben said,

wiping blood off his palm. Ben had never been fond of cats. He'd lost his first hamster to a neighbor's cat, and his current hamster, Snooze, was under constant surveillance by Grandpa Abe's cat. Ben had to keep his bedroom door closed at all times. "What do we do now?"

Ben and Pearl looked around. The first time they landed in the Imaginary World, they'd been greeted by a parched desert. The second trip had brought them to a forest of tangled vines. Today they found themselves on a narrow dirt path that was lined on each side by a row of hedges. But because this was the Imaginary World, these were no ordinary hedges—they grew as tall as trees. Tweets and chirps sounded from the uppermost branches. Globs of bird poop lined the sides of the path like polka dots.

"The sky looks stormy," Ben noted. Gray clouds were gathering over the hedges. "I hope it doesn't rain." His mom wouldn't be pleased if he ruined his new shoes.

Ben looked up the path. It continued on and on toward the horizon. Then he looked back down the path. It kept going as far as the eye could see. "Which way do we go?"

"Hey, Mr. Tabby," Pearl said. "Which way to the palace?"

The cat ignored them and began to clean his other front paw.

"He's not listening," Pearl said. "Do you think he understands? Do you think he's forgotten about Dr. Woo already?"

Ben frowned. That would be a terrible turn of events. "Mr. Tabby, we need to get the feather, remember? Everyone's sick."

The cat's gaze turned upward and focused on a purple songbird that had popped its head out of the hedge. The cat's whiskers trembled.

"I know what to do." Ben pulled a Macker from his pocket and held it by its rubbery tail. "If you lead us to the griffin's palace, I'll give you this." He dangled the treat in front of the cat's face. The cat sniffed, rose onto his hind legs, and batted at the cracker. Ben raised his arm higher, moving the cracker just out of reach.

"Do you think he understands?" Pearl asked.

"I sure hope so." Ben jiggled the cracker. "Take us to the griffin king, and this will be your reward."

The cat flicked his tail, turned, and headed up the road.

"Yay!" Pearl cried. Ben smiled. Maybe this would work out after all.

With Pearl holding the leash and the cat in the lead, they walked for a very long time. Whether on four cat paws or in polished shoes, Mr. Tabby's walk was the same. He took long, graceful steps, held his nose high, and emitted an air of superiority. He stopped occasionally to sniff the broken eggshells that lay here and there, some speckled, some striped. Some even glowed like neon lights. He darted after songbirds if they flew too low. "Cat instincts," Pearl whispered. The sky rumbled as dark clouds continued to gather.

"This road goes on and on and on," Pearl complained.

Indeed, there appeared to be no end. Where was this palace? Ben expected to see turrets rising in the distance, or a drawbridge and moat. But there was nothing but the dirt path and the hedges.

"At least you don't have to walk in these shoes," he grumbled, his toes aching beneath the stiff black leather.

The cat took a sudden right turn, darting out of view. "Hey, wait!" Pearl cried. Then she slipped after the cat. "Oh, cool! Come see this!"

Ben followed, crawling through an opening in the hedge. Once he'd reached the other side, he scrambled to his feet and stood next to Pearl. Stretched before them, the land sloped gently downward, offering a sweeping view of more hedges, growing in geometric patterns.

"It's a maze," Pearl said excitedly. "I've never walked through one. Have you?"

"No," Ben replied. "But I built one for my hamster. It was a science fair project." He'd hypothesized that Snooze would run at different speeds through the maze depending on what sort of food was waiting at the end. A wilted lettuce leaf might not entice, but a beloved cheese puff would surely get his little

legs pumping. The project was a failure, however, because it turned out, no matter what the reward, Snooze had only one speed—sluggish.

Ben and Pearl followed the cat down the hill and into the maze. The cat pranced along, leading them left, then right, then left again. Ben lost all sense of direction and started to feel dizzy. "Are we going in circles?" he asked. Everything looked exactly the same—green hedge walls, broken shells, and polka-dot poop. But then, something different caught his eye. "What's that?"

A sign had been mounted on one of the hedge walls.

"Maximus Steele," Pearl hissed.

"Who else could it be?" Ben asked as he reread the sign. They knew that Maximus was on the loose in the Imaginary World. He'd stolen one of the rain dragon's horns and he'd tried to get a unicorn horn, too. "I hope the king arrests him before he hurts any other creatures."

"I hope he's sent to prison forever," Pearl said with a stomp of her foot. "Then he'll never hurt anything ever again!"

The cat began to hiss. At first, Ben thought Mr. Tabby was adding his disapproval of Maximus Steele. But the cat wasn't looking at the sign. He was looking around the corner of the hedge. His fur stood on end, and he arched his back. A shiver darted down Ben's spine. What was the cat looking at?

Pearl took a peek. "Uh-oh," she said.

"Halt!" a voice bellowed. A spear appeared, pointed at Pearl's chest. Another pointed at Ben's. "By order of the king, you are hereby under arrest!"

Pearl was so startled she dropped the leash.

13

Two satyrs stepped out from behind the hedge. They didn't look anything like Vinny. While he'd been dressed in blue pajamas, these two wore armored vests and chain mail. While Vinny's horns had stuck out of messy black hair, their horns poked out of metal helmets. And while Vinny's beard had been scruffy, theirs were long and braided. Plus, these guys were twice as big, twice as muscular, *and* holding spears.

"Why are we under arrest?" Pearl asked. She didn't look one bit afraid. "We didn't do anything wrong."

The soldier standing closest to Pearl flared his nostrils and snorted. "You're under arrest because you're humaaaaans." The name VLAD was engraved on his vest.

The second soldier, whose spear was aimed directly at Ben, sniffed the air. "That's a human stench, no doubt about iiiiit." The name VIC was engraved on his vest.

"Are you saying we smell bad?" Pearl put her hands on her hips. "That's really rude. I took a bath this morning and used apple shampoo. It's from the Dollar Store, so it's a pretty good deal."

"I like apples," Vlad said. He leaned close and nibbled a strand of Pearl's hair.

"Hey, stop that," she told him, stepping away. He shrugged, then started chewing on the handle of his spear. Just like Violet and Vinny, these satyrs would eat anything!

"What are your naaaaames?" Vic demanded.

"I'm Pearl Petal."

"And you?" Both satyrs glared at Ben. Ben stood

perfectly still as Vic's spear hovered an inch from his chest. The tip looked super sharp.

"B...b...b..." Ben stuttered. "B...b...b..." He sounded like Victoria. Was this how she'd felt after coming face-to-face with the sasquatch? "Ben," he finally managed.

Vlad stopped gnawing on his spear. "As members of the king's guard, we are under orders to arrest the human pooooooacher." He pointed to the WANTED sign. Then, with his big front teeth, he took a bite out of the hedge.

"Oh, now I understand," Pearl said. "Look, we're not poachers. We didn't hurt the rain dragon. We helped it. And we saved the unicorn foal."

"We work for Dr. Woo," Ben explained. "We're her new apprentices."

"Got any proof?" Vlad asked, hedge leaves spraying from his mouth.

Ben stuck a finger under his collar, trying to loosen it. Despite the cloudy weather, he'd broken into a nervous sweat. "Proof?" Unfortunately, neither he nor Pearl had special identification cards, or badges. And they weren't wearing their usual lab coats, either. Ben wiped his forehead with the back of his hand. He'd never been arrested before, and it occurred to him that maybe he should call a lawyer. His dad was a lawyer, but did the Imaginary World have the same laws? The right to representation. The right to make a phone call. Innocent until proven guilty.

Doubtful.

"We can prove we work for Dr. Woo because her assistant came with us," Pearl said. "His name is Mr. Tabby."

Using his spear's handle, Vlad pushed his helmet away from his eyes. "So? Where is he?"

Vic leaned on his spear. "Yeah. Wheeeeere?"

"Where? He's right here. He's…" Pearl turned in a circle. "Uh-oh. Mr. Tabby's gone!"

"What?" Ben gasped. In all the commotion, Ben had forgotten that Pearl had let go of the leash. And during all the spear-pointing, Mr. Tabby had wandered off. "How could you let him get away?" Ben snapped.

"Don't get mad at me," Pearl said. "It's not *my* fault." She got down on her knees and peered under the hedge.

"Of course it's *your* fault." Ben crouched next to her. A neon-green eggshell cracked beneath his palm. "It's totally your fault. You were holding the leash."

"Fine. Blame it on me," she grumbled. "But maybe we should stop arguing and find him. Mr. Tabby! Mr. Tabby!"

She was right. Arguing wouldn't solve any of their problems, which seemed to be piling up. "Mr. Tabby!" Ben looked under another hedge. "Here, kitty, kitty, kitty."

While Ben and Pearl searched frantically for the missing cat, the two soldiers helped themselves to handfuls of leaves. "Where do you wanna get luuuu-unch?" Vlad asked.

"I don't know. Where do you wanna get luuuu-unch?" Vic said, his mouth mostly full.

"Clover sounds good. We could go graze the field."

"We had clover yesterday." Vic snorted. "How about some brambles? Or some baaaaark?"

"What are we going to do?" Ben whispered in Pearl's ear. "We can't summon the Portal without Mr. Tabby. He's got the fairy dust."

"We'll find him," she insisted. "He wouldn't leave us."

"Mr. Tabby *the person* might not leave us," Ben said, "but Mr. Tabby *the cat* would. Remember, he said his cat instincts start to take over, and he forgets about his life with Dr. Woo."

Pearl opened her mouth to say something, then froze. A dark shadow had fallen over the hedge maze. Ben, Pearl, and the soldiers looked up. A massive black cloud had parked itself directly overhead.

"Looks like things are getting worse," Vlad said. "We'd better gooooo."

Vic swallowed, then pointed his spear. "All right, you two. Start marching."

"Marching?" Ben asked. He and Pearl scrambled to their feet. "But we have to find Mr. Tabby."

Vlad shook his head. "Don't try to stall. We've got orders to arrest any humans and take them to the king."

"But—" Ben was about to point out, once again, that he and Pearl were not poachers, when Pearl squeezed his arm real hard. "Ow. Why'd you do that?"

"They want to take us to the king," she whispered. "We need to see him, remember?"

Ben nodded. It would have been so much nicer to arrive at the palace as visitors, rather than prisoners. "Okay."

Vlad took the lead, his hooves stomping the ground as he marched. "Go on," Vic told Ben and Pearl. But Ben hesitated.

"If I turn my back, you're not going to head-butt me, are you?"

"Just because I'm a satyr, you think I head-butt?" Vic asked. "That's offensive."

"Just wondering," Ben said. Then, with Vic's spear pointed at their backs, he and Pearl headed down the path. Ben glanced over his shoulder, hoping to glimpse a flash of reddish-orange fur.

But Mr. Tabby was nowhere to be seen.

14

As the satyr soldiers ushered Ben and Pearl
through the hedge maze, Ben considered the
situation. The good news was, they were heading to the griffin's palace. They didn't need Mr. Tabby
to lead the way after all. The bad news was, Mr.
Tabby was missing.

Before leaving the Portal, Mr. Tabby had told
Ben and Pearl to never let him off the leash. *This
is Pearl's fault*, Ben thought with a sour expression.
Pearl was always, always, always getting them into
trouble. She'd let the leprechaun out of the hospital,
she'd dumped dragon droppings off the roof, and

now she'd dropped the leash and lost Mr. Tabby!

"Here, kitty, kitty, kitty," Pearl called, her hands cupped around her mouth.

"You'd better not say that in front of the king," Vic warned with a grunt.

Ben had to think about that for a moment. It made sense that a lion—even a half lion—wouldn't want to be called "kitty." "Did you hear that?" he whispered to Pearl. "Don't say, 'here, kitty, kitty, kitty' in front of the king. Or you'll get us into more trouble."

"Yeah, okay," Pearl said. "You don't have to be so snippy."

They turned left, then right, then left again, passing another WANTED sign.

"How much longer before we can talk to the king?" Ben asked the soldiers. "We've got to find Mr. Tabby *and* get back by three o'clock. That's when we're expected home." And that's when they'd start to help cure everyone of Troll Tonsillitis. Hopefully.

"Talk to the king?" Vlad snorted. "You hear that, Vic? They want to *taaaaalk* to the king."

"What's the matter with you two?" Vic asked.

"Don't you know it's a bad-mood day?" He pointed to the sky. Storm clouds continued to brew.

"What's a bad-mood day?" Ben asked.

"If the king's in a good mood, it's sunny and warm at the palace. If he's in a sad mood, it rains. If he's in a bad mood, well, it's miiiiiserable." Thunder sounded and a lightning bolt seared a nearby hedge.

"Whoa!" Ben said, nearly jumping out of his dress shoes. "That was close!"

"Why's the king in a bad mood?" Pearl asked as the smoke cleared.

"The riddles have run out," Vlad said.

Pearl laughed. "That doesn't make sense. You can run out of milk and bread, but how can you run out of riddles?"

"The king's heard them aaaaall," Vic told her. "And no one's been able to find any new ones."

"Well, I bet Ben can help. He's super good at making things up." Pearl smiled at Ben. Ben didn't smile back. Mr. Tabby had said that the best way to make a griffin happy was to engage in a battle of riddles. Ben hoped this wouldn't come to pass. It was one thing to make up a story for Pearl or Grandpa Abe, but for the king of the entire Imaginary World? Talk about serious pressure!

"Here we aaaaare," Vlad announced.

They'd reached the end of the maze. A massive golden gate stood before them, gleaming despite the lack of sunlight. A pair of golden lion paws held the gate closed, while a pair of golden wings rose above it. Tall hedges flanked the gate, and a flag waved from atop a pole. The gray flag bore the image of a griffin. "That's the bad-mood flaaaaag," Vlad said.

"Maybe you should get one," Pearl whispered to Ben. "Then I'd know when you're going to be cranky."

"Cranky?" Ben exclaimed. "I'm only cranky because *you* dropped the leash." He would never have dropped the leash. At least, that was what he told himself. "Anyway, it doesn't matter what kind of mood *I'm* in," Ben pointed out. "You should be worried about the king. If he's in a bad mood, he might not give us a feather. And don't forget that his rating on the danger scale depends on his mood."

The storm clouds rumbled.

Vlad reached up and unhooked one of the golden paws. The gate swung open. Ben steadied himself, preparing to be awed. Surely the king of the Imaginary World lived in a palace more magnificent than anything he'd read about in storybooks. Or anything he could create in one of his own stories.

But what he saw was a tree.

Sure, it was a pretty big tree, with a trunk as broad as a house. The branches reached so wide, they blocked out the angry gray sky. A narrow wooden staircase wound up the tree, disappearing into the dense foliage.

Pearl looked around and said the exact same thing that Ben was thinking. "Where's the palace?"

"You're looooooking at it." Vlad pointed to the base of the tree, which had been hollowed out like a cave.

"It's a den," Ben realized. This made total sense. He'd been expecting a traditional castle, with turrets, a moat, and a drawbridge. But the king was half lion, and lions lived in dens.

Ben and Pearl followed Vlad across a lush grass carpet. A group of satyr soldiers were sitting together, eating brown-bag lunches. They waved at Vlad and Vic.

"I'm so excited," Pearl said as she grabbed Ben's arm. "I don't care that I had to wear a skirt, and I don't care that we've been arrested. We get to meet another king!" As she smiled, her steps became extra bouncy.

Ben returned the smile, though his was more clenched. Pearl never seemed to focus on the bad or dangerous stuff. Ben wished he could be more like her. On the other hand, being cautious could help keep them safe. If the griffin king's bad mood elevated him to a five-plus on the danger scale, Pearl and Ben would be in for a heap of trouble. So, while Pearl bounced around, giddy with anticipation, Ben was determined to stay focused and on alert.

"We're going inside," she said with a squeal as Vlad led them into the hollowed-out tree.

A throne, with lion's feet at the base and wings

sprouting from the top, had been carved from the tree itself. Ben's gaze darted immediately to a pile of discarded bones that lay at the base of the throne. Clearly the griffin king was a carnivore. Fortunately, none of the bones belonged to anything larger than a rat.

"Where's the king?" Pearl asked.

"He's holding a meeting in his neeeeest." Vlad pointed upward.

"A nest *and* a den," Ben said. "That makes sense."

Vic prodded Ben's shoulder with his spear, pushing him toward a wooden pen that looked like a cage. "Since you're both under arrest, you'll await your trial in there."

"Trial?" *Uh-oh.* Maybe they needed a lawyer after all. "I'd like to make my one phone call," Ben said. "I want to call Dr. Woo and let her know what's going on." While he'd never seen a phone in the Imaginary World, he knew that it was somehow possible to call the switchboard and report an emergency. The unicorn king had called when his foal went missing.

"No calls without authorization from the king."
Vlad pointed at the cage. "Inside, both of yooooou."

"No way am I going in there," Pearl said, folding her arms tightly. "Besides, you don't need to put us on trial, because we're not poachers. How many times do we have to tell you that?"

"Can't we just talk to the king?" Ben asked. "We'll make it real quick, and then he can get back to his meeting." But a head-butt from Vic landed Ben in the cage. Vic was about to butt Pearl, too, but she waved her hands.

"Okay, okay, no need to get pushy." She stepped inside voluntarily. Vlad closed and locked the cage door.

"Let's get some lunch," Vlad said.

"Yeah, I'm practically staaarving."

"Don't forget to tell the king we're here!" Pearl called as Vlad and Vic left the den.

Ben rattled the door. It held tight. "We're in jail, Pearl. Jail."

"It's not jail," she said. "It's just a big birdcage.

Besides, even if there is a trial, we're innocent. This is a simple misunderstanding." She hiked up her skirt and adjusted her basketball shorts. "Anyway, what we should be worried about is getting a griffin feather, so my parents will stop looking like Mr. and Mrs. Potato Head."

"I wonder how long we're going to have to wait," Ben said. He started to think of ways to break out, just in case. They could dig a tunnel, or maybe Pearl was skinny enough to squeeze between the bars.

"Look!" Pearl exclaimed.

A reddish-orange cat pranced into the den, his nose held high as if he owned the place. A vial of yellow fairy dust sparkled at his neck. The leash, which was still attached to his harness, dragged behind him. The cat wasn't lost after all. He'd been following them this whole time. *What a relief!* "Hi, Mr. Tabby," Ben said.

The cat ignored him. He stood on his hind legs and proceeded to sharpen his claws on the side of the throne. "Does that seem like a rude thing to do?"

Ben asked Pearl. After all, it was a king's throne, not a scratching post.

"It does seem a bit rude."

Ben was worried that Mr. Tabby's behavior would put the king in an even worse mood. He snapped his fingers. "Hey, Mr. Tabby, stop doing that."

Pearl patted her knee. "Here, kitty, kitty, kitty."

Still ignoring them, the cat leaped onto the throne, then sharpened his claws on one of the carved wings. "Oh, that's bad. Bad kitty," Ben scolded. The cat flicked his tail, his claws digging into the wood. Then he raised his tail even higher and aimed his rear end at the corner of the throne.

"Oh no!" Ben cried. "He's going to spray. We've got to stop him!"

"Here, kitty, kitty, kitty. *Here, kitty, kitty, kitty!*" Pearl yelled, her voice echoing throughout the den.

From far above came the sound of creaking branches.

Luckily, the cat didn't spray. He lowered his tail and looked up at the ceiling. More branches creaked. The entire tree shuddered. Without a glance at the apprentices, the cat leaped off the throne and dashed away.

Before Pearl could ask any questions, and before Ben could do any worrying, a sharp wind blew across their faces. Then a huge bird flew into the den and landed on the dirt floor. It opened its hooked beak, but it didn't tweet or chirp or caw.

It roared.

15

Ben's heartbeat drummed in his ears and his legs trembled—for good reason. He was face-to-face with one of the most magnificent creatures he'd ever seen.

While the rain dragon had been grand in size, the griffin was grand in design. His back half was covered in sleek fur, golden and glossy. His long tail ended in a dark tuft, like a pom-pom. His front half was feathered, the plumage chocolate brown with a golden sheen around the neck. As he tucked his wings, he stared at Ben and Pearl with a piercing gaze. Then his beak opened.

"Who so dareth to disturbeth my meeting?" The voice was just as Ben had expected from such a noble creature—deep in tone, royal in diction. And grumpy. Definitely grumpy.

"I guess I did," Pearl admitted.

"So did I," Ben said. Pearl might have shouted the loudest, but she shouldn't take all the blame. They'd both been trying to get Mr. Tabby's attention.

The king reached up with one of his front legs, which ended in talons, and adjusted his jeweled crown. "I was meeting with my most trusted advisor. I do not liketh to be disturbed." A clap of thunder sounded outside.

"We're sorry," Pearl said. Then she added, "Your Majesty." She leaned forward. "Bow," she whispered to Ben from the corner of her mouth. He bowed so quickly, his forehead clunked against the cage. Formal dress and formal manners were supposed to please the griffin king. But when Ben straightened, the king did not look any happier.

"Guards!" he bellowed. Vlad and Vic ran into the den. One carried a half-eaten branch, the other a handful of vines. They fell to their knees. The king glanced down at them. "Why have I foundeth two human children in my den?"

"We are obeying Your Majesty's command," Vlad reported. "To bring you any humans we find. The boy and the girl were in your maze."

The feathers around the king's ears bristled. "Did I heareth correctly? They were trespassing in my maze?"

"Yes, Your Majesty," Vlad said.

"Do you want us to take them to the pit?" Vic asked. Stringy bits of vine hung from his beard.

"The pit?" Ben cried. If Vic had used the word *hole* Ben wouldn't have reacted so fiercely. A hole didn't sound too bad. Toads lived in holes. But vipers lived in pits. A hole was where you planted a rosebush or buried a pet hamster. But a pit conjured all sorts of ugly images, like bubbling lava and consuming darkness. "Okay, wait a minute. This is a huge mistake. We weren't trespassing. We—" The griffin king took a quick step forward. He stood so close to the cage that Ben could see his own reflection in the king's eagle eyes.

"Have we met beforeth?" the king asked.

"No," Ben said with a gulp.

"Then it is cleareth that I did not giveth you permission to exploreth my maze. Therefore, thou art a trespasser."

Ben didn't like the sound of that statement. Trespassing was against the law back home. But the truth was, they hadn't gotten permission to walk through the maze. "Dr. Woo sent us," Ben said. He was about to explain, but Pearl was quicker. She pressed her face against the cage, aiming her words between the bars.

"Dr. Woo sent us because she has Troll Tonsillitis, and so do the sasquatch, Metalmouth, Violet, and my parents, and Victoria, and half the town by now. We need one of your feathers because it's the only cure."

"That's right," Ben said. "We're not poachers. We'd never hurt anyone or anything."

Pearl smiled. "It's really nice to meet you, Your Majesty. I've only met one other king. I like your crown."

While Vlad chewed on his branch as if it were a carrot stick, and Vic swallowed another mouthful of vines, the king continued to glare at Ben and Pearl, his tail flicking with annoyance. "How do I knoweth that you speaketh the truth?"

"Oh, we do speaketh, I mean, *speak* the truth," Ben said.

"You gotta believe us," Pearl pleaded. "If you call Dr. Woo, she'll tell you that we're her brand-new apprentices. This is Ben and my name's—"

"Waiteth!" the king hollered. The word echoed throughout the den. "Do not speaketh your name. Riddle it instead."

Pearl shuffled in place. "You want a riddle for my name?" She turned to Ben and whispered, "I don't know a riddle for my name."

"We'd better think of one," Ben whispered back.

"And maketh sure that it be a good riddle," the king said. "The riddles have runneth out, and I am in need of new ones."

Ben closed his eyes and tried to clear his head. *Don't worry about Mr. Tabby*, he told himself. *Don't worry about being put in a pit or being kept in the Imaginary World forever. Don't worry about what will happen if you and Pearl can't bring back a feather.* Ben tried to remember what Mr. Tabby had told them. A joke had a punch line, but a riddle had an answer. And the answer to this riddle was Pearl.

Images flooded Ben's mind. He saw an actual pearl. It was round and gleaming. It looked like a full moon. Then he saw his father buying a strand of pearls for his mother. Then he saw the oyster shell that sat on the jewelry store's counter. Pearls grew in oysters. *That was it!* Ben's eyes flew open.

"I have a riddle, Your Majesty." Ben took a long breath. This was an important moment. If the riddle pleased the king, then he might let them out of the cage. Ben folded his hands behind his back. "Her name begins with a grain of sand."

"Oooh, that's good," Pearl said with a smile.

The griffin king whipped his tail as if trying to swat a fly. Then he cleared his throat. "The answer doth be Pearl."

"Yes!" Pearl cried.

Vlad and Vic applauded. The king walked over to his throne and sat with a loud "*Hmmph.*" He perched his feathered elbows on the armrests. "It doth be a good riddle, but I am stilleth in a beastly mood."

Pearl gripped the cage bars. "Ben's in a bad mood, too."

"I am not," Ben insisted.

Pearl rolled her eyes. "Yes, you are. You're mad because I dropped Mr. Tabby's leash. But that's not the only reason. You were already in a bad mood when you came to work this morning."

Ben didn't say anything. He did *not* want to talk about that other reason.

"Speaketh," the king ordered. "Why was thou in

a bad mood on this morn?" Vlad and Vic stopped eating. Their goat ears pricked up.

Pearl whispered in Ben's ear. "Talk to him. We need to gain his trust so we can get a feather."

The king tapped his talons together. "I do not liketh to be kept waiting!"

Ben fidgeted. He knew he could make up a story. He could say he felt grumpy because he'd found a dead moth in his cereal. Or because a troupe of clowns had stolen his comfortable shoes. "Well," he began, "you see, Your Majesty, I'm..." He was stalling. Pearl elbowed him. *Gain his trust.* Ben knew trust couldn't be gained with a lie. That made no sense. Trust had to be gained with truth. His shoulders slumped. "I felt bad this morning because I found out that my mom and my dad are going to live in two different houses."

Sometimes it felt better to let a secret fly free, but this time it felt worse.

"Oh, Ben, I'm so sorry," Pearl said, patting his back.

The griffin king unfolded his hands and sat up

straight. "Thou art sad because thou willst haveth two homes? But I haveth two homes. I haveth my den and I haveth my nest."

Ben leaned against the cage. "You like living in two places?"

"Yes, I doth liketh it very much. The den is niceth on stormy days. The nest is niceth on sunny days. The nest is whereth I discuss. The den is whereth I ponder." He narrowed his eyes. "But I haveth nothing to ponder because the riddles haveth run out."

"Do you want Ben to tell you another riddle?" Pearl asked. "If he does, can we have one of your feathers to take back to Dr. Woo?" Ben and Pearl clung to the cage bars, waiting for the king's reply.

"Very well. If your riddle doth maketh me ponder and doth maketh me pleased, then I shall giveth you a feather."

16

A ROYAL RIDDLE

The griffin king wanted a riddle. Not just any riddle. It had to make him ponder, and it had to make him pleased.

"Okay, Your Majesty," Pearl said. "It's a deal. A riddle for a feather. Ben can do it. He's a fantastic storyteller."

Ben scratched his head. He'd already made up the riddle about Pearl's name. Now he had to come up with another one? He was used to making up stories when he wanted to get out of doing chores, or because he'd forgotten to do his math homework, but he'd never had to do it while locked in a cage. Or with the threat of being thrown into a pit.

Pearl smiled at Ben. She looked deep into his eyes. No one had ever looked at him with such confidence. There wasn't a drop of doubt on her face. "You can do this."

A riddle for a king? Ben furrowed his brow, trying to squeeze an idea out of his brain. What should the riddle be about? While he wondered, Vlad and Vic made themselves more comfortable. They set their spears aside and sat crisscross on the dirt floor. Vlad reached under his helmet and pulled out an ear of corn. Vic reached under his helmet and pulled out a pear. Did satyrs ever stop eating?

"Do not keepeth me waiting!" the king bellowed. "I haveth important matters to tendeth to."

"Okay, okay," Ben grumbled. *Yeesh*. The griffin king was acting as if he was the most important

person in the world. Maybe he was. *That's it*, Ben realized. Because the king thought himself so important, the riddle should be about him. The answer would be *king*. Now, to create the question. Thanks to Ben's morning at the senior center yesterday, something popped to mind immediately. "Okay, I've got one, Your Majesty."

The griffin king gripped his throne. "Proceedeth."

Ben cleared his throat. And this was his riddle:

THE WEAKEST IN CHESS
BUT THE STRONGEST IN CHECKERS.
WHO AM I?

The griffin king clicked his beak. "Chess? Checkers? Thou doth speaketh words I do not knoweth." His voice grew louder. "I am most displeased."

"Shall I throw him in the pit, Your Majesty?" Vlad asked.

"Uh-oh," Pearl said between clenched teeth.

"You're making the king even grumpier, Ben. Think of something else."

Ben was pretty sure that having *king* as the answer would please the griffin. He'd try again. His gaze darted around the den. What things belonged to the king? There was the crown that circled his head, and the tall wooden throne. Words swirled through Ben's head. "I have one, Your Majesty." And this is what Ben recited:

A HAT WITH NO END
THAT MARKS HIS GRACE.
A CHAIR WITH NO BEND
THAT HOLDS HIS PLACE.
WHO IS HE?

The king said not a word. He nodded, then closed his eyes, retreating into thought. Except for the sounds of the satyr soldiers eating their snacks, the den filled with silence. Pearl squeezed Ben's arm. Ben shuffled in place, his stomach churning with

anxiety. He'd forgotten all about his uncomfortable shoes and his stifling dress shirt. All that mattered was the king's reaction. Would this riddle get them a feather?

Or doom them?

The king slowly opened his eagle eyes. He clicked his beak three times, then reached up and took the golden crown off his head. He held it out and ran a talon around it. "'A hat with no end that marks his grace.'" Then he patted an armrest. "'A chair with no bend that holds his place.'" He paused. "The answer be, the king."

"Yes," Ben said.

Vlad and Vic applauded. "Excellent, Your Majesty!"

Pearl smiled, then whispered in Ben's ear. "Oh, that was a good one. You're so clever." But Ben was still worried. Had the riddle been too easy to solve?

The griffin king stood, then slowly walked toward the cage, his intense gaze never faltering. Ben swallowed hard. The king's chest feathers bristled as he stood in front of Ben, the razor-sharp beak pointed directly at him. "I liketh being the answer to a riddle. Thou doth pleaseth me."

The opening to the den began to glow as a beam of sunlight appeared outside.

"Can we have the feather now?" Pearl asked.

The king sat on his furry haunches. "The riddle round is not complete. It is my turn to asketh you." And this is what he said:

**WHETHER ONE OR TWO,
THOU SHALT FIND
IT IS NOT A PLACE
BUT A STATE OF MIND.**

The phrase *state of mind* felt very familiar to Ben. He'd heard someone use it recently. Yesterday morning, in fact. And the someone had been Metalmouth. The dragon had told Ben and Pearl that when he got sad about moving away from home, Dr. Woo said that home was a *state of mind*.

Ben looked into the griffin king's eyes. Was this creature, half eagle and half lion, trying to make him feel better? "Home," Ben said quietly.

The king nodded. "Well doneth." Then he strode to the den's entrance, his crown glinting in the streaming sunlight. "Soldiers!"

Vlad and Vic leaped to their hooves. "Yes, Your Majesty!"

"My mood hath improved," the king announced. "Change the flag."

The soldiers bowed. "Thy will be done," they both said, then hurried away.

"My trusted advisor shall attendeth to your needs," the king told Ben and Pearl. "I must taketh to the sky to hunteth for my lunch."

"But, Your Majesty!" Pearl called. "You said you'd give us a feather for a riddle."

"If thou looketh above and not behind, what thou seeketh so thou shalleth find."

"Another riddle?" Ben asked, his shoulders slumping.

"The riddle will leadeth thou to a feather," the king explained.

"But aren't you going to let us out of this cage?" Pearl asked. "So we can look?"

"I agreed to giveth thou a feather, but I never agreed to releaseth thou from the cage." The griffin king chuckled, a glint in his eye. "Today thou hast made me happy. I shall keepeth thou to be my royal riddlers." He strode out of the den, his tail swaying gracefully.

"Keep us?" Ben cried, his voice cracking. His worst fear had come true. He and Pearl were trapped in the Imaginary World—forever!

A rhythmic sound arose as wings began to beat air. Ben and Pearl pressed against the cage, trying to catch a glimpse of the griffin king as he flew away.

"This is totally unfair!" Pearl said with a stomp of her foot. "He can't leave us here!"

"He's the king. He can do anything he wants," Ben said. He reached through the bars, pulling at

the lock. "We have to get out of here. I can't become a royal riddler. My parents are going to get really mad if I don't come home at the end of summer." The lock held fast. Ben tried squeezing between the bars, but he was too big. Pearl tried, but she couldn't fit, either.

"What are we going to do?" she asked.

"You are going to leave this world and never come back," someone said. Ben and Pearl gasped.

A man stood in the den's entrance.

17

THE TRUSTED ADVISOR

Even though he'd never met the man, Ben knew in his gut that he was face-to-face with Maximus Steele. What other human would be in the Imaginary World, dressed like a big-game hunter?

Maximus's cargo pants were tucked into sturdy black hiking boots. His short-sleeved khaki shirt had multiple pockets and a matching vest. A knife hung from a belt that looked to be made of snake or crocodile skin, but could have been from an Imaginary creature. A pith helmet and a pair of binoculars completed the outfit.

Ben glanced at Pearl to judge her reaction. She'd seen Maximus before, when she'd been sent into the Tangled Forest to find the missing unicorn foal. While hiding in the darkness, Maximus had descended on the back of a giant moth. He'd set up a trap, then he'd flown away. Pearl had jammed the trap with a tree branch, ruining Maximus's chances of getting a unicorn horn that day. But she never got a look at his face.

"It's him," she whispered to Ben. "I can tell."

"I think you're right," Ben whispered back.

"What a lovely day," Maximus said. He stood in the den's entrance, sunlight filling the space behind him as if a spotlight had been turned on to announce his arrival. "The storm clouds have disappeared."

Ben scowled. He wasn't interested in a weather report. What was Maximus Steele, the notorious poacher, doing at the griffin king's palace?

With slow, confident steps, Maximus walked up to

the throne and sat. Then he leaned back, stretching his long, skinny legs. For the first time since being arrested, Ben was glad to be locked in a cage. A wall of bars separated him from the most dangerous man in the Imaginary World. He and Pearl were trapped, but they were safe. For now.

Maximus took off his helmet, and Ben and Pearl got to see his face. It wasn't as evil as Ben had imagined. There was no eye patch, no hooked nose or pockmarked skin. His hair was dark and cropped super short, like Ben's. He had a wide nose and almond-shaped eyes.

"I presume you are Emerald's new apprentices?"

Ben wasn't used to hearing someone call Dr. Woo by her first name. But he remembered that she and Maximus had grown up together. They'd been best friends as kids.

"How about we ask *you* the questions?" Pearl said, jutting out her chin. "What are you doing here?"

"Didn't the king tell you?" Maximus laughed wickedly. "I am his trusted advisor."

"How can the king trust you? You're the one who hurt the rain dragon," Ben said. "He should arrest you. Not us!"

Maximus balanced his pith helmet on his knee. "The king is blissfully unaware of my true occupation."

"You mean you lied to him," Pearl said. "I'm going to tell him the truth. You're a poacher. You take horns."

"Not just horns. Anything of value that a collector might buy." He tapped his fingers on his helmet. "Sea serpent skin makes a lovely waterproof tent. Yeti fur protects against the coldest weather. And nothing is sharper than dragon teeth. They make superior knives." He pulled his knife from its sheath. Ben and Pearl stepped backward, deeper into the cage. "But the griffin king doesn't know my true nature. I told him that I'm a dear friend of Emerald's. And I know a few riddles, so it was easy to earn his trust."

"But there's a WANTED sign in the maze," Ben said. "For a dangerous human poacher."

"I blamed the poaching on someone else," Maximus said.

"Who?"

His voice turned icy. "There is someone else in this world, someone who has been trying to stop me." He stood and took a step toward the cage. "I worked very hard to lure a unicorn foal, but a branch was jammed into my trap, ruining my plan. No footprints were left at the scene, so I have no proof who damaged my trap. But I have my suspicions."

Ben glanced at Pearl's feet. During her adventure in the Tangled Forest, she'd been wearing her leprechaun shoes. They allowed her to move in total silence. Apparently, they didn't leave footprints.

Maximus stood very close to the cage. "You wouldn't know anything about what happened in the Tangled Forest, would you?" He looked directly at Pearl. She gulped.

At that moment, Ben was grateful that Mr. Tabby had made them dress up for their visit to the griffin's palace. Because the yellow ribbon that Pearl was wearing in her hair was covering an important clue. After saving the unicorn foal, Pearl and Ben had been given strands of unicorn mane, and the strands had magically attached themselves to their heads. Anyone who knew anything about unicorns would recognize the white stripes as proof of membership in an elite organization called the Order of the Unicorn. Ben's stripe was hidden under hair at the nape of his neck, but Pearl's was usually easier to spot. Thanks to the yellow ribbon, Maximus couldn't see the white stripe. He couldn't know, for certain, that Pearl had been rewarded by the unicorn king.

"We don't know what you're talking about," Ben lied. "We've never been to the Tangled Forest. Dr. Woo sent us here because she's sick."

"Sick?" Maximus Steele's expression softened. "How sick?"

"She has Troll Tonsillitis," Pearl said. "And she won't get better without a—"

"A griffin feather," Maximus interrupted. "Of course." With his knife still clasped in his hand, he took a sudden, angry swing at the lock. It split open and fell to the ground. Ben and Pearl stumbled backward until they were pressed up against the cage's back wall. Maximus yanked open the door. What was he going to do?

"Go on," he said with a sweep of his arm. "Before the king returns."

Ben wasn't going to argue. He rushed out, Pearl at his heels. "Why did you do that?" he asked when they were free.

Maximus returned his knife to its sheath. "You may think me cold-hearted, but I care about Emerald. She was very kind to me when we were children. I don't want her to be sick. Go get the griffin feather so that she may be cured." He grabbed his pith helmet and set it on his head. "But give her this message. If she is the one tampering with my traps, she had best stop, or I will no longer consider her to be my friend. And I will tell the griffin

king to forbid her from entering this world."

"But the creatures need Dr. Woo," Pearl said. "Who will take care of them if they get sick?"

Maximus chuckled. "If creatures get sick, then they weaken. And weak creatures are easier to catch."

"You can't do that," Ben said.

"I can do whatever I want. I'm the king's *trusted advisor.*" And then, after a tip of his hat, Maximus Steele exited the den. None of the lunching satyrs tried to stop him as he hurried out the golden gate, disappearing into the hedge maze.

"I don't care that he set us free. I still don't like him," Pearl said.

Ben was relieved that he wasn't going to be living in a cage, making up riddles for the rest of his life. But the feeling was fleeting. "We have to get the feather, find Mr. Tabby, and summon the Portal before the king comes back."

"Yeah, but where's the feather?"

Ben repeated the riddle. "If thou looketh above

and not behind, what thou seeketh so thou shalleth find." He chewed on his lower lip. "If we look above we'll find what we seek." He and Pearl both looked up at the den's ceiling.

"The nest!" they exclaimed.

18

Ben and Pearl tiptoed out of the den. None of the satyr soldiers noticed the escape. Vlad and Vic were too busy grazing on the lawn, and the other soldiers had their noses buried deep in their lunch bags.

The tree's staircase was much steeper than the one that led to the tenth floor of Dr. Woo's hospital. Halfway up, Ben's legs began to burn as if his muscles had caught fire. "Don't look down," he warned after doing just that. He closed his eyes for a moment, fighting a dizzy spell. Then he opened them and continued climbing.

"I can't believe we met Maximus Steele," Pearl said. "Dr. Woo's going to be surprised when we tell her."

"And angry," Ben said. They had a lot of bad news to deliver. Maximus had not only gained the griffin king's trust, but he'd also threatened to keep Dr. Woo out of the Imaginary World forever.

Round and round they went. The branches grew thicker, blocking the view. Ben had no idea how far they'd climbed. Then he bumped into Pearl. She'd stopped walking because they'd reached the top. "Wow," he said.

The royal nest was perched in the tree's uppermost branches. Unlike Metalmouth's nest, which was made of metal forged by the dragon's fiery breath, the griffin's nest was woven from sticks. And it was the size of Grandpa Abe's living room.

"Can you imagine if I added this to my collection?" Pearl asked. Ben had seen Pearl's bird-nest

collection. She kept it in her bedroom, which sat right above the Dollar Store. There was no way she could get this nest through the front door.

"Look," Pearl said. She walked to the center of the nest and picked up a feather. Not an ordinary feather, but one that was golden and the size of an oar. "It's light," she said, surprised.

"Really?" Ben couldn't believe it. Cautiously, he stepped into the nest, testing each branch before letting it bear his full weight. A few creaks and groans sounded, but the woven branches held tight. Ben took the feather from Pearl's hands. "Amazing. It weighs less than a piece of toast."

Pearl shielded her eyes with her hand and looked at the sweeping view. "This is great. I wish I could live up here. My bed would fit, and my dresser, and most of my stuff."

Ben wanted to sit down because the height was making him dizzy again. But what a view it was. Beneath the sun-kissed sky, the golden gate gleamed and a yellow good-mood flag rippled in a gentle breeze. To the right, the hedge-lined path stretched as far as the eye could see. To the left, a dense forest grew, dappled with cool shadows. And straight ahead, a tapestry of rolling hills sparkled yellow, like fairy dust.

"Do you think that's where the fairies live?" Pearl asked.

"Makes sense," Ben said. How odd that question would have sounded if he'd heard it a week and a half ago, before he'd known anything about the Imaginary World. He checked the sky for signs of the griffin king. If the king discovered that they'd escaped, he'd surely put them back into the cage. Hopefully, the king's hunting would take a while longer. "We'd better get going. We still have to find—"

"Meow."

"Mr. Tabby?" Ben and Pearl darted around. A speck of color peeked through a patch of leaves. Ben hurried to the nest's edge and pushed the leaves aside. Sure enough, a tabby cat was clinging to the end of a branch, his eyes wide with fear. The hair on

his back stood up like bristles on a scrubbing brush. Ben was happy to see that Mr. Tabby was alive and well. He was equally happy to see the vial of fairy dust safely tied around the cat's neck.

Ben had never owned a cat, but he knew that while they were good at climbing *up* trees, they were terrible at coming down. The fire department had visited his neighborhood last summer to help get Mr. Fluffy, a prize-winning Himalayan, out of a palm tree. Luckily, the firefighter had been wearing protective gear because that cat had gone ballistic with the hissing and scratching.

"Hold on," Pearl said. She climbed out of the nest, then stepped onto the branch. She took three steps before the branch creaked. Then it started to crack.

"Watch out!" Ben cried, pulling her back into the nest. The cat growled as the branch wobbled. The leash dangled from his harness, swaying in midair.

"Drat!" Pearl said. "How are we going to get him?" She opened her mouth real wide and hollered, "*Here, kitty—*"

Ben put his hand over her mouth. "Don't do that! Last time we yelled, 'Here, kitty, kitty, kitty,' the griffin king heard us, remember?"

Pearl nodded. Then she moved Ben's hand from her face. "But how are we going to get him off that branch?" she asked. "We can't let him fall. That would be so sad. Poor Mr. Tabby." Was that a tear in her eye?

The cat did not look one bit happy. He spat and hissed and growled all at once. "If we had a cat toy, or a treat, or..." Ben reached into his pocket and pulled out a Macker. "I forgot about these." He held it by its rubbery tail. "Look, Mr. Tabby! Look what I have. Yummy." The cat paid no attention to Ben. He dug his claws into the bark, holding on for dear life. The Macker didn't work.

"I'm gonna have to climb out there," Ben said. Then he winced. Had those words actually come out of his mouth?

"Really?" Pearl asked. "Do you think it's safe?"

Ben had never heard Pearl ask that particular question. He suspected she'd never asked it before in her entire life. And the fact that she'd chosen *this* moment to do so made him feel very worried. But Ben ignored that feeling. He'd been learning to do that lately.

The branch that jutted out from the trunk, just below the cat's branch, looked to be much thicker. Perhaps it could hold Ben's weight. He removed his tie. "Distract him with this." Pearl took the tie, then flicked it around like a piece of yarn. The cat slowly turned his head, watching the tie as if hypnotized.

Ben walked four steps down the staircase, then climbed onto the thicker branch. *Don't look down*, he told himself. Scooting on his bottom, he inched his way forward until he was directly below the cat. *I can't believe I'm doing this*, he thought. Sitting on the end of a branch, high above the ground, certainly contradicted every cautious instinct in Ben's body. But there was a saying he'd heard about throwing caution to the wind. Seemed this was the right time to do just that.

"Good kitty," Pearl said soothingly. As the cat shifted position, his branch cracked again. He hissed and spat, his yellow eyes filling with wild terror. The end of the leash dangled just above Ben's head. "Hurry," Pearl told Ben. "He's freaking out!"

"*He's* freaking out?" Ben's entire body had broken into a cold sweat. Gripping his branch with his left hand, he reached out with his right, fingertips barely brushing the dangling leash. The cat's ears flattened and he began to whimper. Ben stretched as far as he could. "I...can't..." If only he could make his fingers grow another inch. He took a deep breath and stretched again. There it was! With the leash's handle clasped in his fingers, he gave a quick yank. The cat toppled off the branch, right into Ben's outstretched arms.

"Woo-hoo!" Pearl yelled, which was immediately followed by, "Oh no!" Because the branch Ben and the cat were on broke!

19

MR. TABBY AGAIN

Ben wasn't sure what had happened, because when you're falling out of a tree, there's not much time to think. But once it was all over, Pearl told him exactly what she had seen.

Apparently, when the cat landed in Ben's arms, the additional weight was just enough to crack the thicker branch, sending both Ben and the cat on a downward tumble. However, when the cat landed in Ben's arms, the impact also broke the vial of fairy dust, summoning the Portal.

The tornado's appearance was instantaneous. For a moment, the swirling wind cradled Ben and the cat in midair. Then, as its momentum grew, it pushed the pair right back into the tree. They landed, unharmed, on the staircase.

"Ben!" Pearl called. She stumbled down the stairs, dragging the feather behind her. The wind tore the bow out of her hair. "You did it," she said, beaming her gap-toothed smile. "You saved Mr. Tabby."

The cat growled and squirmed. Even though Ben felt a bit stunned, he held on to the cat with all his strength. "You're not getting away this time," he grumbled in the cat's ear.

With a clap of thunder, the Portal touched down at the tree's base. Gale-force winds continued to push against Ben and Pearl, making their descent slow and difficult. Branches swayed, and leaves ripped free. The staircase shuddered. "We're almost there!" Pearl cried. When they reached the ground, Pearl didn't hesitate. Feather in hand, she ran straight into the tornado. Ben didn't give it a second

thought. With his arms wrapped tightly around the cat, he followed.

As he staggered into the Portal's interior room, the relief was immediate. No more wind in his face, no more worry about finding the vial of fairy dust. The griffin king hadn't returned, Maximus Steele was gone, and the feather had been found. As Ben relaxed his grip, the cat jumped to the floor. But he didn't touch down with four furry paws. Rather, he landed in a pair of shiny black shoes. The leash and harness fell away.

"Mr. Tabby," Pearl said. "Welcome back."

He was dressed, once again, in perfectly creased pants, a crisp white shirt, and a metallic gold vest. The only evidence of his adventure was the broken vial hanging from the cord around his neck.

"We got the feather," Pearl told him.

"And we met Maximus Steele," Ben added. There was so much to say. Where should he begin? "He wants us to give a message to Dr. Woo."

"Destination, please," the captain's voice interrupted.

After smoothing his vest and tucking in his shirt-tail, Mr. Tabby cleared his throat. "Dr. Woo's Worm Hospital." Then he made an *ack* sound and picked a couple of reddish-orange hairs off his tongue.

"Setting coordinates for Dr. Woo's Worm Hospital. Please fasten your seat belts and prepare for takeoff."

As the Portal began to vibrate, Ben pressed his heels into the floor to keep his balance. As usual, the ride was bumpy. Ben might have been focused on the bone-rattling turbulence. He might have been worried about falling out into unexplored dimensions. But instead he watched Mr. Tabby. The doctor's assistant had not said a word to Pearl or Ben. He hadn't looked at them, either. Ben didn't expect a thank-you for saving the cat's life, but he did want some sort of recognition that the mission had been successful. Was Mr. Tabby upset that they'd allowed him to wander off leash?

No one spoke again until they'd landed safely on the tenth floor. Even Pearl refrained from asking questions. She held the feather, never taking her eyes off Mr. Tabby.

"Destination reached," the captain announced.

"I think we might be in trouble," Pearl whispered to Ben. Ben nodded.

The Portal disappeared and the fairy dust settled. Ben was happy to see that Vinny wasn't there to greet them—or to *head-butt* them. A note taped to the switchboard read:

SNACK BREAK.
BACK SOON.

Pearl looked a mess. Her skirt had been torn by tree branches, her ribbon was gone, and her hair looked as if it had been styled by a squirrel. Ben, likewise, was a disaster. His shirt was ripped, his tie was loose, and fresh cat claw marks glistened on his hands.

"Wow, that was a crazy trip," Pearl said.

Mr. Tabby raised an eyebrow. "I wouldn't know. I have no memory of the journey."

"Seriously?" Pearl blew a strand of hair from her eyes. "You don't remember that you sharpened your claws on the king's throne and climbed a tree and got stuck?"

"A detailed report is unnecessary," he said with a dismissive wave. "What I do when I am in feline form does not concern me. I trust that my cat instincts took over and I acted as a cat should. I also trust that you did not let me wander."

"Uh..." Ben's mouth fell open. "We got the feather. Isn't that what really matters?" If Mr. Tabby didn't want details, then Ben wasn't going to volunteer details. Why get in trouble unnecessarily? He looked at his watch. "It's two forty-five," he said. "My grandpa's coming to get me at three."

Mr. Tabby's mustache twitched. "Then we must make haste."

Downstairs, in the Identification Room, Mr. Tabby chopped the feather into pieces and pulverized them in a blender. He opened the plaid thermos and poured Grandpa Abe's matzo ball soup into four bowls. Then he sprinkled powdered griffin feather into each bowl, stirring until the flakes dissolved. "I shall serve these to Dr. Woo, Metalmouth, Violet, and the sasquatch. But I shall rely on you to take care of the Buttonville residents. Can you manage?"

"Yes," Ben said. "But wait. We need to see Dr. Woo. We have to give her Maximus Steele's message."

"I do not wish to upset the doctor at this time. She is ill and needs her rest." Mr. Tabby set the four bowls of soup on a tray.

Pearl stepped in front of him and launched into an explanation, her words flying out at jet speed. "But Maximus is lying to the griffin king. He's pretending that someone else is doing the poaching. The king trusts him. We were arrested and put in jail. Those goats were going to throw us in a pit! The king wanted to keep us forever because the riddles have run out. Maximus broke the lock and set us free because he cares about Dr. Woo. But then he gave us a warning. He said that if Dr. Woo keeps

tampering with his traps, he'll tell the king to forbid her from entering the Imaginary World. And then who would take care of the creatures?" Her face had turned red. She gasped for breath.

"Yeah," Ben added. "Exactly what she said."

Mr. Tabby looked deep into Pearl's eyes and then into Ben's. "These are not matters that should concern two human children. The best way you can help Dr. Woo at this time is to cure your townspeople of Troll Tonsillitis before it becomes an international news item. Is that clear?"

Ben and Pearl nodded.

Mr. Tabby handed Ben three things: a vial of powdered griffin feather, Grandpa Abe's empty thermos, and a small tube labeled CAT SCRATCH CREAM.

20

They worked late into the night. After kicking off her shredded skirt, Pearl collected a bunch of thermoses from the Dollar Store. While Grandpa Abe made batch after batch of his famous matzo ball soup, Ben and Pearl filled the thermoses. And when Grandpa Abe wasn't looking, they sprinkled each one with the magical cure.

Using a Food 4 Less shopping cart, Ben and Pearl delivered the thermoses all over Buttonville, stopping first to help Pearl's parents. The change was immediate. Faces and necks deflated. Sore throats returned to normal. Everyone was amazed by the soup's healing properties. "Be sure to thank Abe," they all said. "That's the best soup ever."

But one house in particular they saved for last.

The little red wagon was parked outside. Pearl knocked on the front door, but no one answered.

"Maybe they're asleep," Ben whispered. It was late and most of the windows in the house were dark. "We could wait until morning."

"It's tempting," Pearl said. "But as much as I don't like Victoria, we have to cure her or she'll just keep spreading the sickness." She yawned. "Besides, I'm really tired. I want to go to bed."

"Me too," Ben said. The door was unlocked, so they tiptoed inside.

The Mulberry house was clean and tidy, with shoes lined up in a perfect row and not a single dish in the sink. A pair of binoculars sat on each window-sill, and a telescope was pointed out the front picture window. Two red baseball caps hung on pegs, along with two sets of red overalls.

Loud snoring led them upstairs to Mrs. Mulberry's

bedroom. Her frizzy red hair was tucked beneath an old-fashioned nightcap. Her flannel nightgown was buttoned all the way to her chin. Her face looked perfectly normal.

"She must not have tonsils," Ben whispered. He was glad they didn't have to wake her. As she slept, she clutched a pair of binoculars to her chest and mumbled, "You can't hide from me, Dr. Woo." Then she started snoring again.

Victoria was in the next room in a pink canopy bed, resting her big, swollen head on a pink pillow. Her nightlight cast a warm glow throughout the room. She moaned when Ben and Pearl stepped inside. "B...b...big. F...f...furry," she mumbled.

"We don't know what you're talking about," Ben told her. He opened the thermos and poured the soup into the cup-shaped lid. Then he handed it to Pearl.

"Drink this," Pearl told Victoria. "It'll make you feel better." She held the cup to Victoria's lips.

With a loud slurp, Victoria drank some soup. And right before Ben's and Pearl's eyes, the magical transformation occurred, accompanied by the distinct sound of a balloon deflating. Victoria's hands flew to her face.

"I'm normal again!" she exclaimed. She bolted upright. "I can talk!" She grabbed her glasses off the bedside table, slid them up her nose, then pointed a finger at Ben. "Don't tell me you don't know what I'm talking about. Big and furry—that's what I saw!"

"You were imagining things," Ben said.

"No, I wasn't." Victoria crossed her arms and glared at them. "It was big. It was furry. And it smelled really bad. Like a wet dog. Or sweaty socks."

Pearl laughed in a fake way. "Are you telling us that you saw a monster?" She laughed again. "Monsters aren't real."

"Then what was it?" Victoria asked.

Pearl nudged Ben, waiting for him, once again, to make up a good story.

"Well," he said, "monsters aren't real. But your brain thinks it saw one because...because...Did you get a good look at your head? It was the size of a watermelon. Of course you thought you saw a monster. Your brain was squished."

Victoria frowned. "I guess that makes sense. But what about the dragon? I saw him before I got sick. You know it's true." She sank into her frilly pillows. "It's so boring following Mom around while she does her snooping. I want to have fun. I want to meet a dragon."

If Ben hadn't been so tired, he might have felt a wee bit sorry for Victoria. But all he could do at that moment was yawn. Then he rubbed his eyes. "We gotta get going."

"You can keep the thermos," Pearl said as she and Ben hurried from Victoria's room.

"I won't give up!" Victoria shouted after them. "I'm going to meet that dragon whether you help me or not!"

Ben and Pearl couldn't get down those stairs fast enough. As they darted toward the front door, they almost tripped over two boxes. One contained the compost worm that Mr. Tabby had cured. The other contained the rest of the compost worms that Mrs. Mulberry had ordered from a specialty gardening catalog.

"They don't even have a compost pile," Pearl said with a frown. "I'll set them free in the park on my way home." After closing the front door, she placed both boxes into the shopping cart. "Well, I guess this is good night."

"Yeah," Ben said, yawning again.

"As soon as Dr. Woo gets better, we need to tell her what happened with Maximus Steele."

"Definitely."

As the stars twinkled above, Pearl put her hand on Ben's shoulder. "I'm sorry I said you needed a bad-mood flag."

"That's okay. I'm sorry I got mad at you for dropping the leash."

They were too tired to say anything more. So off Pearl went, pushing the cart toward Main Street and the Dollar Store.

As Ben headed in the other direction, the first rays of dawn peeked over the trees. Grandpa Abe was waiting for him on the front porch, slowly rocking on the cherry-red swing.

"Did you deliver all the soup?" Grandpa Abe asked.

"Yes," Ben said. "I think everyone's going to be okay."

"That's good news." He handed a bowl to Ben. "You'd better have some. To make sure you don't get sick, too."

Ben didn't argue. He was pretty hungry. So he sat next to his grandfather and ate two entire bowls.

"Oh, I almost forgot." Grandpa Abe held out a note card. "That odd man with the funny mustache came by and delivered this." Ben read the card.

Dear Mr. Silverstein,

Thank you for your lovely soup. It made me feel much better. Someday I would like to get the recipe, for it is wondrous soup indeed.

Sincerely,
Dr. Emerald Woo

"You see, I told you my soup cures everything." Grandpa Abe chuckled. Then he leaned back and promptly fell asleep.

Ben stretched out his legs and folded his arms behind his head. His bad mood was definitely gone. Maybe his grandfather's soup had made him feel better. But so had the wise words from the griffin king. What Ben had come to realize was this— whether home was in a tree, in a den, with a mother, or with a father, what made a place home was how Ben looked at it.

Life back in Los Angeles was going to be different, that was for certain. But different was plenty good.

CERTIFICATE OF MERIT

__BEN SILVERSTEIN__

IS HEREBY SKILLED IN THE ART OF

CURING A GRIFFIN KING'S GRUMPINESS

CERTIFICATE OF MERIT

__PEARL PETAL__

IS HEREBY SKILLED IN THE ART OF

CURING A GRIFFIN KING'S GRUMPINESS

PUT YOUR IMAGINATION
☷ TO THE TEST ☷

The following section contains writing, art, and science activities that will help readers discover more about the mythological creatures featured in this book.

These activities are designed for the home and the classroom. Enjoy doing them on your own or with friends!

CREATURE CONNECTION
★ *Griffin* ★

When you take the king of beasts and combine him with the king of birds, you get the most majestic creature of all—the griffin. With the body, tail, and back legs of a lion, and the head, wings, and front legs of an eagle, the griffin is a powerful force on land and in the air. And that is why the griffin has been a symbol of divine power across different cultures.

One of the earliest images of this regal beast was found in the ruins of a famous palace called Knossos, on the Greek island of Crete. There, in the throne room, beautiful murals of griffins can still be seen today. Other ancient civilizations, such as Egypt and Persia, also included griffins in their art and stories. During medieval times, a knight bearing a griffin on his coat of arms was thought to be a courageous and bold leader.

According to legend, a griffin chooses only one mate, and if that mate dies, the griffin lives out the rest of its life alone. This sounds sad, but poets found this very romantic. It was also said that griffins love gold and fiercely guard their treasures. Their claws and feathers were believed to heal certain diseases and conditions, including blindness. Medieval merchants made a lot of money selling goblets made from griffin claws (actually antelope horns) and selling delicious griffin eggs (actually ostrich eggs).

Where did the idea of a half-lion, half-eagle creature come from? One theory is that the creature is based on a dinosaur called protoceratops. If people from ancient times stumbled across the fossilized remains of this dinosaur, they could have easily mistaken the creature for being half bird because it had a very large neck frill and a jaw that was so big it looked like a beak. The body of the protoceratops was the size of a sheep and had four legs. Skeletons of protoceratops have been found in many different

places, and this might explain why many different cultures came up with similar stories about a half-beast, half-bird creature.

Today, the griffin's image is used to promote many products. The car company Saab uses a griffin in its logo, as does the professional hockey team the Grand Rapids Griffins. Many colleges and schools use a griffin, including Trinity College in Oxford, England.

Of course, we can't always know exactly where an idea comes from. That's the mystery of story-telling.

STORY IDEAS

Imagine that you are living a very long time ago and that your father is a traveling merchant. You've just arrived in a new village, ready to sell your goods. The people are simple and have never traveled beyond their hamlet, so they are amazed by the things you have in your wagon. How do you convince the villagers that the "griffin" eggs are real, even if they look a lot like chicken eggs?

★ ★ ★ ★ ★

It's a special day at the palace of the griffin king and queen. Their first baby is being hatched. You've been invited to witness and celebrate this event. Describe your experience.

ART IDEA
Can you draw a griffin? Remember that the front is all feathered, with an eagle's face and bird legs and talons. The back half is furry, with back legs that end in paws and a long lion's tail. Don't forget the pair of wings.

CREATURE CONNECTION
⋆ *Bakeneko* ⋆

Have you ever noticed that cats are mysterious creatures? Unlike friendly dogs, who beg for affection, like to hang out with their owners, and come when they're called, cats can be standoffish, often preferring solitude, and are talented at ignoring their owners. There's a saying that we own dogs, but cats own us.

Long ago in Japan, people also thought that cats were mysterious creatures. They believed that even though a cat might live with people, it still possessed the soul of a wild animal. The legend of the bakeneko was born. This creature might look like an ordinary cat, but it was able to shape-shift into human form, and would act in a mischievous manner. While in cat form, the bakeneko could speak human language and walk on hind legs. But the strangest thing of all—it liked to put a napkin on its head and dance. Super weird, right?

How did this story arise? Well, there are a few theories. In ancient Japan, people used lanterns that were fueled by oil. Mostly, this oil was made from fish. The village cats were like cats all over the world. They craved fish, and so they could often be found licking oil from the lanterns. In order to do this, the cats had to stand up on their hind legs to reach the oil. While licking the oil, the light would shine on their faces, making them look quite wicked. Storytellers are always looking for interesting things to write about—and so, ordinary cats standing on hind legs became magical, transforming cats.

It was also said that a cat could become a bakeneko if its tail grew very long. Because no one wanted to own a wicked shape-shifting cat, it became common practice to cut off the tails of cats. After centuries of this practice, today there is a breed of cat with a very short tail—the Japanese bobtail.

The idea that cats can do weird things was not limited to Japan. In ancient China, it was said that a cat could bewitch humans, especially a white-tailed cat. Thus, white cats were not popular. One of the most powerful cats in mythology is the Egyptian goddess Sekhmet, whose face is that of a lioness.

So remember, your pet kitty might be sleeping peacefully on the couch, but if you suddenly can't find your dinner napkin, don't be surprised if your cat is wearing it on its head and dancing around the living room.

STORY IDEAS
What would you do if your cat started talking to you in a human language? Would you freak out? Would you laugh? Does your cat have something important to tell you? Create a story based on this idea.

ART IDEAS
Draw a picture of what you'd look like as a cat. Doesn't that sound like fun? Are you long-haired or short-haired? Are you orange, striped, black, or white? Do you wear a fancy rhinestone collar, or do you live on your own in the wild?

SCIENCE CONNECTION
⋆ *All About Feathers* ⋆

We all know what a feather is, right? Feathers are those things that stick out of a bird. Sometimes they are stuffed into pillows. Sometimes they tickle us and make us sneeze.

But did you know that feathers are amazing feats of engineering? They do much more than make a bird look pretty. They help a bird fly, which is probably their most important function. They provide thermal insulation, which means they keep a bird warm. They also provide waterproofing. Have you ever heard the saying "like water rolling off a duck's back"? Now you know what that means.

Ever wonder why the female mallard duck is covered in plain brown feathers while the male mallard duck has lots of color? Her feathers help her blend into the surrounding forest while she's sitting on her nest, taking care of her eggs. Providing camouflage is another function of feathers.

There are different types of feathers. Baby birds are born with downy feathers that fall out and are replaced. Vaned feathers have hollow tubes that grow from the skin. These tubes are called quills, and we sometimes use them for writing. Bristle feathers are found around eyes and beaks.

Feathers have tiny hairs called barbules. These barbules hook together. They allow feathers to be airtight for flying and watertight for floating.

We've found many different ways to use feathers. Goose down jackets and comforters keep us warm. Feathered fishing lures help us catch fish. And arrows fly straighter if they're made with feathers. In India, peacock feathers are used in traditional medicines. Eagle feathers are important to Native Americans. They are symbols of honor and usually given to a tribal member after an act of bravery or a good deed. To be given an eagle feather is especially important because the eagle is considered to be the leader of all birds.

So the next time you take a walk and find a

feather lying in the grass, pick it up and give it a careful look. Remember that it not only helps a bird look beautiful, but it also provides flight, insulation, and waterproofing. It's one of nature's most amazing creations.

CREATIVITY CONNECTION
⋆ *Make a Worm Compost Bin* ⋆

If you live out in the country, or have a big back-yard, it's pretty easy to make a compost pile. But for those of us who live on city lots or in apartment buildings, how can we make compost dirt with very little space and just scraps from our kitchen?

First, what is compost? It's a rich, dark brown dirt that's left when organic material (leaves, sticks, flowers, etc.) decays. You can speed up this process by having worms do most of the work.

Here's how to create a worm compost bin.

1. Get a wooden or plastic box with a tight-fitting lid, to keep out pests. Drill holes in the bottom for drainage. Place the bin in a shady part of yard, maybe up on bricks to help with draining.

2. Fill the bin with bedding, such as leaves, sawdust, and/or shredded newspapers. The most important thing is to make sure the bedding is moist, so spray it with a hose or spritz it with a bottle. Throw in a handful of dirt to help the worms digest their food.

3. Add some worms. Make sure you get red worms, not fishing worms such as night crawlers and garden worms. Where can you get these red worms? Well, if your friend has a compost pile already, ask if you can dig some out. Or you can order them like Mrs. Mulberry did.

4. Once the worms are in place, you can start adding your food scraps. Don't add kitchen scraps that are animal-based, such as meat or dairy, because they take a long time to break down and will attract rats. Also, you will get maggots if you add meat. Yuck!

Things you can add include tea bags, coffee grounds, greens, fruits, bread, grains, newspaper, cardboard, and leaves.

5.   After you add the scraps, mix them into the bedding. Put moist newspaper over the top to keep out the flies and to keep the soil moist so the worms are happy.

6.   As the lovely compost dirt is made, push it to one side of the bin and add food scraps to the other side. Now you can use the dirt whenever you like.

CREATIVITY CONNECTION
★ *Write a Riddle* ★

Riddles are questions that are tricky to answer. They are puzzling on purpose. That is why they are so much fun. For example: *What gets wetter and wetter the more it dries?* Answer: *A towel.* Here's another example: *I'm black and white and read all over. What am I?* Answer: *A newspaper.*

If you'd like to create your own riddles, here are some steps that might help.

1. Start with the answer. Make it something that everyone is familiar with. For example, let's choose *cat.* Now that you have the answer, begin working on the question.

2. Create a list of words and phrases, everything you can think of that describes

your answer. Use a thesaurus to help with
some words you might not have thought of.

Furry
Four paws with claws
Whiskers
Purring sounds
Long, swishing tail

3. Now think about your answer in other ways.
    How does it feel to be the answer? How does
    it smell or taste? What does it do or want?
    Think of some phrases that use *like* or *as*.

    Likes to hunt at night
    Wants to eat mice
    Wants to sleep in sunbeams
    Wants to nap all day
    Quiet as the night
    Prowls like a shadow
    Plays with yarn
    Hates water!

Here is a riddle for *cat*:

OUT OF SIGHT, IN THE NIGHT,
WAITING FOR A MOUSE DELIGHT.
WHO AM I?

Now you try.

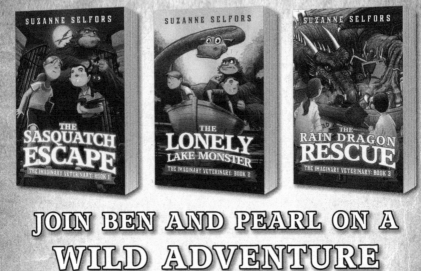

Wecome to Ever After High!

Don't miss the first book in a new series! In *Next Top Villain*, Lizzie Hearts and Duchess Swan compete for top honors in General Villainy class—who will win?

Ever After High
Next Top Villain

Suzanne Selfors

Ever After High
GENERAL VILLAINY
A DESTINY DO-OVER DIARY
Companion to *NEXT TOP VILLAIN!*

Suzanne Selfors

Also check out *General Villainy: A Destiny Do-Over Diary*—the companion hextbook filled with activities straight out of the *Next Top Villain* story! Take General Villainy class with your favorite characters and rewrite the story: Accept thronework assignments from Mr. Badwolf, help Lizzie and Duchess choose different destinies, and more!

Find out more about Ever After High books at **everafterhigh.com**